Henry James OM (15 April 1843 – 28 February 1916) was an American-British author regarded as a key transitional figure between literary realism and literary modernism, and is considered by many to be among the greatest novelists in the English language. He was the son of Henry James Sr. and the brother of renowned philosopher and psychologist William James and diarist Alice James.

He is best known for a number of novels dealing with the social and marital interplay between émigré Americans, English people, and continental Europeans. Examples of such novels include The Portrait of a Lady, The Ambassadors, and The Wings of the Dove. His later works were increasingly experimental. In describing the internal states of mind and social dynamics of his characters, James often made use of a style in which ambiguous or contradictory motives and impressions were overlaid or juxtaposed in the discussion of a character's psyche.(Source: Wikipedia)

Literary works:
Watch and Ward (1871)
Roderick Hudson (1875)
The American (1877)
The Europeans (1878)
Confidence (1879)
Washington Square (1880)
The Portrait of a Lady (1881)
The Bostonians (1886)
The Princess Casamassima (1886)
The Reverberator (1888)
The Tragic Muse (1890)
The Other House (1896)
The Spoils of Poynton (1897)
What Maisie Knew (1897)

PRINCE CLASSICS

THE MADONNA
OF
THE FUTURE

HENRY JAMES

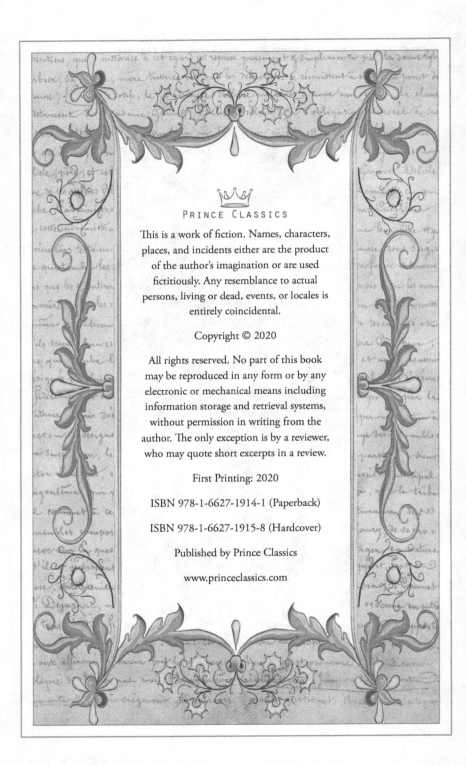

PRINCE CLASSICS

First Printing: 2020

ISBN 978-1-6627-1914-1 (Paperback)

ISBN 978-1-6627-1915-8 (Hardcover)

Published by Prince Classics

www.princeclassics.com

Contents

THE MADONNA
OF
THE FUTURE

THE MADONNA OF THE FUTURE

We had been talking about the masters who had achieved but a single masterpiece—the artists and poets who but once in their lives had known the divine afflatus and touched the high level of perfection. Our host had been showing us a charming little cabinet picture by a painter whose name we had never heard, and who, after this single spasmodic bid for fame, had apparently relapsed into obscurity and mediocrity. There was some discussion as to the frequency of this phenomenon; during which, I observed, H--- sat silent, finishing his cigar with a meditative air, and looking at the picture which was being handed round the table. "I don't know how common a case it is," he said at last, "but I have seen it. I have known a poor fellow who painted his one masterpiece, and"—he added with a smile—"he didn't even paint that. He made his bid for fame and missed it." We all knew H--- for a clever man who had seen much of men and manners, and had a great stock of reminiscences. Some one immediately questioned him further, and while I was engrossed with the raptures of my neighbour over the little picture, he was induced to tell his tale. If I were to doubt whether it would bear repeating, I should only have to remember how that charming woman, our hostess, who had left the table, ventured back in rustling rose-colour to pronounce our lingering a want of gallantry, and, finding us a listening circle, sank into her chair in spite of our cigars, and heard the story out so graciously that, when the catastrophe was reached, she glanced across at me and showed me a tear in each of her beautiful eyes.

* * * * *

It relates to my youth, and to Italy: two fine things! (H--- began). I had arrived late in the evening at Florence, and while I finished my bottle of wine at supper, had fancied that, tired traveller though I was, I might pay the city a finer compliment than by going vulgarly to bed. A narrow passage wandered darkly away out of the little square before my hotel, and looked as if it bored into the heart of Florence. I followed it, and at the end of ten minutes emerged upon a great piazza, filled only with the mild autumn moonlight. Opposite rose the Palazzo Vecchio, like some huge civic fortress, with the great bell-tower springing from its embattled verge as a mountain-pine from the edge of a cliff. At its base, in its projected shadow, gleamed certain dim sculptures which I wonderingly approached. One of the images, on the left of the palace door, was a magnificent colossus, shining through the dusky air like a sentinel who has taken the alarm. In a moment I recognised him as Michael Angelo's *David*. I turned with a certain relief from his sinister strength to a slender figure in bronze, stationed beneath the high light loggia, which opposes the free and elegant span of its arches to the dead masonry of the palace; a figure supremely shapely and graceful; gentle, almost, in spite of his holding out with his light nervous arm the snaky head of the slaughtered Gorgon. His name is Perseus, and you may read his story, not in the Greek mythology, but in the memoirs of Benvenuto Cellini. Glancing from one of these fine fellows to the other, I probably uttered some irrepressible commonplace of praise, for, as if provoked by my voice, a man rose from the steps of the loggia, where he had been sitting in the shadow, and addressed me in good English—a small, slim personage, clad in a sort of black velvet tunic (as it seemed), and with a mass of auburn hair, which gleamed in the moonlight, escaping from a little mediæval birretta. In a tone of the most insinuating deference he asked me for my "impressions." He seemed picturesque, fantastic, slightly unreal. Hovering there in this consecrated neighbourhood, he might have passed for the genius of æsthetic hospitality— if the genius of æsthetic hospitality were not commonly some shabby little custode, flourishing a calico pocket-handkerchief and openly resentful of the divided franc. This analogy was made none the less complete by the brilliant tirade with which he greeted my embarrassed silence.

"I have known Florence long, sir, but I have never known her so lovely as tonight. It's as if the ghosts of her past were abroad in the empty streets. The present is sleeping; the past hovers about us like a dream made visible. Fancy the old Florentines strolling up in couples to pass judgment on the last performance of Michael, of Benvenuto! We should come in for a precious lesson if we might overhear what they say. The plainest burgher of them, in his cap and gown, had a taste in the matter! That was the prime of art, sir. The sun stood high in heaven, and his broad and equal blaze made the darkest places bright and the dullest eyes clear. We live in the evening of time! We grope in the gray dusk, carrying each our poor little taper of selfish and painful wisdom, holding it up to the great models and to the dim idea, and seeing nothing but overwhelming greatness and dimness. The days of illumination are gone! But do you know I fancy—I fancy"—and he grew suddenly almost familiar in this visionary fervour—"I fancy the light of that time rests upon us here for an hour! I have never seen the David so grand, the Perseus so fair! Even the inferior productions of John of Bologna and of Baccio Bandinelli seem to realise the artist's dream. I feel as if the moonlit air were charged with the secrets of the masters, and as if, standing here in religious attention, we might—we might witness a revelation!" Perceiving at this moment, I suppose, my halting comprehension reflected in my puzzled face, this interesting rhapsodist paused and blushed. Then with a melancholy smile, "You think me a moonstruck charlatan, I suppose. It's not my habit to bang about the piazza and pounce upon innocent tourists. But tonight, I confess, I am under the charm. And then, somehow, I fancied you too were an artist!"

"I am not an artist, I am sorry to say, as you must understand the term. But pray make no apologies. I am also under the charm; your eloquent remarks have only deepened it."

"If you are not an artist you are worthy to be one!" he rejoined, with an expressive smile. "A young man who arrives at Florence late in the evening, and, instead of going prosaically to bed, or hanging over the traveller's book at his hotel, walks forth without loss of time to pay his devoirs to the beautiful, is a young man after my own heart!"

The mystery was suddenly solved; my friend was an American! He must have been, to take the picturesque so prodigiously to heart. "None the less so, I trust," I answered, "if the young man is a sordid New Yorker."

"New Yorkers have been munificent patrons of art!" he answered, urbanely.

For a moment I was alarmed. Was this midnight reverie mere Yankee enterprise, and was he simply a desperate brother of the brush who had posted himself here to extort an "order" from a sauntering tourist? But I was not called to defend myself. A great brazen note broke suddenly from the far-off summit of the bell-tower above us, and sounded the first stroke of midnight. My companion started, apologised for detaining me, and prepared to retire. But he seemed to offer so lively a promise of further entertainment that I was indisposed to part with him, and suggested that we should stroll homeward together. He cordially assented; so we turned out of the Piazza, passed down before the statued arcade of the Uffizi, and came out upon the Arno. What course we took I hardly remember, but we roamed slowly about for an hour, my companion delivering by snatches a sort of moon-touched æsthetic lecture. I listened in puzzled fascination, and wondered who the deuce he was. He confessed with a melancholy but all-respectful head-shake to his American origin.

"We are the disinherited of Art!" he cried. "We are condemned to be superficial! We are excluded from the magic circle. The soil of American perception is a poor little barren artificial deposit. Yes! we are wedded to imperfection. An American, to excel, has just ten times as much to learn as a European. We lack the deeper sense. We have neither taste, nor tact, nor power. How should we have them? Our crude and garish climate, our silent past, our deafening present, the constant pressure about us of unlovely circumstance, are as void of all that nourishes and prompts and inspires the artist, as my sad heart is void of bitterness in saying so! We poor aspirants must live in perpetual exile."

"You seem fairly at home in exile," I answered, "and Florence seems to me a very pretty Siberia. But do you know my own thought? Nothing is so idle as to talk about our want of a nutritive soil, of opportunity, of inspiration, and all the rest of it. The worthy part is to do something fine! There is no law in our glorious Constitution against that. Invent, create, achieve! No matter if you have to study fifty times as much as one of these! What else are you an artist for? Be you our Moses," I added, laughing, and laying my hand on his shoulder, "and lead us out of the house of bondage!"

"Golden words—golden words, young man!" he cried, with a tender smile. "'Invent, create, achieve!' Yes, that's our business; I know it well.

Don't take me, in Heaven's name, for one of your barren complainers—impotent cynics who have neither talent nor faith! I am at work!"—and he glanced about him and lowered his voice as if this were a quite peculiar secret—"I'm at work night and day. I have undertaken a *creation*! I am no Moses; I am only a poor patient artist; but it would be a fine thing if I were to cause some slender stream of beauty to flow in our thirsty land! Don't think me a monster of conceit," he went on, as he saw me smile at the avidity with which he adopted my illustration; "I confess that I am in one of those moods when great things seem possible! This is one of my nervous nights—I dream waking! When the south wind blows over Florence at midnight it seems to coax the soul from all the fair things locked away in her churches and galleries; it comes into my own little studio with the moonlight, and sets my heart beating too deeply for rest. You see I am always adding a thought to my conception! This evening I felt that I couldn't sleep unless I had communed with the genius of Buonarotti!"

He seemed deeply versed in local history and tradition, and he expatiated *con amore* on the charms of Florence. I gathered that he was an old resident, and that he had taken the lovely city into his heart. "I owe her everything," he declared. "It's only since I came here that I have really lived, intellectually. One by one, all profane desires, all mere worldly aims, have dropped away from me, and left me nothing but my pencil, my little note-book" (and he tapped his breast-pocket), "and the worship of the pure masters—those who were pure because they were innocent, and those who were pure because they were strong!"

"And have you been very productive all this time?" I asked sympathetically.

He was silent a while before replying. "Not in the vulgar sense!" he said at last. "I have chosen never to manifest myself by imperfection. The good in every performance I have re-absorbed into the generative force of new creations; the bad—there is always plenty of that—I have religiously destroyed. I may say, with some satisfaction, that I have not added a mite to the rubbish of the world. As a proof of my conscientiousness"—and he stopped short, and eyed me with extraordinary candour, as if the proof were to be overwhelming—"I have never sold a picture! 'At least no merchant traffics in my heart!' Do you remember that divine line in Browning? My little studio has never been profaned by superficial, feverish, mercenary work. It's a temple of labour, but of leisure! Art is long. If we work for ourselves, of course we must hurry. If we work for her, we must often pause. She can wait!"

This had brought us to my hotel door, somewhat to my relief, I confess, for I had begun to feel unequal to the society of a genius of this heroic strain. I left him, however, not without expressing a friendly hope that we should meet again. The next morning my curiosity had not abated; I was anxious to see him by common daylight. I counted upon meeting him in one of the many pictorial haunts of Florence, and I was gratified without delay. I found him in the course of the morning in the Tribune of the Uffizi—that little treasure-chamber of world-famous things. He had turned his back on the Venus de' Medici, and with his arms resting on the rail-mug which protects the pictures, and his head buried in his hands, he was lost in the contemplation of that superb triptych of Andrea Mantegna—a work which has neither the material splendour nor the commanding force of some of its neighbours, but which, glowing there with the loveliness of patient labour, suits possibly a more constant need of the soul. I looked at the picture for some time over his shoulder; at last, with a heavy sigh, he turned away and our eyes met. As he recognised me a deep blush rose to his face; he fancied, perhaps, that he had made a fool of himself overnight. But I offered him my hand with a friendliness which assured him I was not a scoffer. I knew him by his ardent *chevelure*; otherwise he was much altered. His midnight mood was over, and he looked as haggard as an actor by daylight. He was far older than I had supposed, and he had less bravery of costume and gesture. He seemed the quiet, poor, patient artist he had proclaimed himself, and the fact that he had never sold a picture was more obvious than glorious. His velvet coat was threadbare, and his short slouched hat, of an antique pattern, revealed a rustiness which marked it an "original," and not one of the picturesque reproductions which brethren of his craft affect. His eye was mild and heavy, and his expression singularly gentle and acquiescent; the more so for a certain pallid leanness of visage, which I hardly knew whether to refer to the consuming fire of genius or to a meagre diet. A very little talk, however, cleared his brow and brought back his eloquence.

"And this is your first visit to these enchanted halls?" he cried. "Happy, thrice happy youth!" And taking me by the arm, he prepared to lead me to each of the pre-eminent works in turn and show me the cream of the gallery. But before we left the Mantegna he pressed my arm and gave it a loving look. "*He* was not in a hurry," he murmured. "He knew nothing of 'raw Haste, half-sister to Delay!'" How sound a critic my friend was I am unable to say, but he was an extremely amusing one; overflowing with opinions, theories, and sympathies, with disquisition and gossip and anecdote. He was a shade too sentimental for my own sympathies, and I fancied he was rather too fond of superfine discriminations and of discovering subtle intentions in shallow places. At moments, too, he plunged into the sea of metaphysics, and floundered a while in waters too deep for intellectual security. But his abounding knowledge and happy judgment told a touching story of long attentive hours in this worshipful company; there was a reproach to my wasteful saunterings in so devoted a culture of opportunity. "There are two moods," I remember his saying, "in which we may walk through galleries— the critical and the ideal. They seize us at their pleasure, and we can never tell which is to take its turn. The critical mood, oddly, is the genial one, the friendly, the condescending. It relishes the pretty trivialities of art, its vulgar cleverness, its conscious graces. It has a kindly greeting for anything which looks as if, according to his light, the painter had enjoyed doing it—for the little Dutch cabbages and kettles, for the taper fingers and breezy mantles of late-coming Madonnas, for the little blue-hilled, pastoral, sceptical Italian landscapes. Then there are the days of fierce, fastidious longing—solemn church feasts of the intellect—when all vulgar effort and all petty success is a weariness, and everything but the best—the best of the best—disgusts. In these hours we are relentless aristocrats of taste. We will not take Michael Angelo for granted, we will not swallow Raphael whole!"

The gallery of the Uffizi is not only rich in its possessions, but peculiarly fortunate in that fine architectural accident, as one may call it, which unites it—with the breadth of river and city between them—to those princely chambers of the Pitti Palace. The Louvre and the Vatican hardly give you such a sense of sustained inclosure as those long passages projected over street and stream to establish a sort of inviolate transition between the two palaces of art. We passed along the gallery in which those precious drawings by eminent hands hang chaste and gray above the swirl and murmur of the yellow Arno, and reached the ducal saloons of the Pitti. Ducal as they are, it must be confessed that they are imperfect as show-rooms, and that, with their deep-set windows and their massive mouldings, it is rather a broken light that reaches the pictured walls. But here the masterpieces hang thick, and you seem to see them in a luminous atmosphere of their own. And the great saloons, with their superb dim ceilings, their outer wall in splendid shadow, and the sombre opposite glow of mellow canvas and dusky gilding, make, themselves, almost as fine a picture as the Titians and Raphaels they imperfectly reveal. We lingered briefly before many a Raphael and Titian; but I saw my friend was impatient, and I suffered him at last to lead me directly to the goal of our journey—the most tenderly fair of Raphael's virgins, the Madonna in the Chair. Of all the fine pictures of the world, it seemed to me this is the one with which criticism has least to do. None betrays less effort, less of the mechanism of success and of the irrepressible discord between conception and result, which shows dimly in so many consummate works. Graceful, human, near to our sympathies as it is, it has nothing of manner, of method, nothing, almost, of style; it blooms there in rounded softness, as instinct with harmony as if it were an immediate exhalation of genius. The figure melts away the spectator's mind into a sort of passionate tenderness which he knows not whether he has given to heavenly purity or to earthly charm. He is intoxicated with the fragrance of the tenderest blossom of maternity that ever bloomed on earth.

"That's what I call a fine picture," said my companion, after we had gazed a while in silence. "I have a right to say so, for I have copied it so often and so carefully that I could repeat it now with my eyes shut. Other works are of Raphael: this *is* Raphael himself. Others you can praise, you can qualify, you can measure, explain, account for: this you can only love and admire. I don't know in what seeming he walked among men while this divine mood was upon him; but after it, surely, he could do nothing but die; this world had nothing more to teach him. Think of it a while, my friend, and you will admit that I am not raving. Think of his seeing that spotless image, not for a moment, for a day, in a happy dream, or a restless fever-fit; not as a poet in a five minutes' frenzy—time to snatch his phrase and scribble his immortal stanza; but for days together, while the slow labour of the brush went on, while the foul vapours of life interposed, and the fancy ached with tension, fixed, radiant, distinct, as we see it now! What a master, certainly! But ah! what a seer!"

"Don't you imagine," I answered, "that he had a model, and that some pretty young woman—"

"As pretty a young woman as you please! It doesn't diminish the miracle! He took his hint, of course, and the young woman, possibly, sat smiling before his canvas. But, meanwhile, the painter's idea had taken wings. No lovely human outline could charm it to vulgar fact. He saw the fair form made perfect; he rose to the vision without tremor, without effort of wing; he communed with it face to face, and resolved into finer and lovelier truth the purity which completes it as the fragrance completes the rose. That's what they call idealism; the word's vastly abused, but the thing is good. It's my own creed, at any rate. Lovely Madonna, model at once and muse, I call you to witness that I too am an idealist!"

"An idealist, then," I said, half jocosely, wishing to provoke him to further utterance, "is a gentleman who says to Nature in the person of a beautiful girl, 'Go to, you are all wrong! Your fine is coarse, your bright is dim, your grace is *gaucherie*. This is the way you should have done it!' Is not the chance against him?"

He turned upon me almost angrily, but perceiving the genial savour of my sarcasm, he smiled gravely. "Look at that picture," he said, "and cease your irreverent mockery! Idealism is *that*! There's no explaining it; one must feel the flame! It says nothing to Nature, or to any beautiful girl, that they will not both forgive! It says to the fair woman, 'Accept me as your artist friend, lend me your beautiful face, trust me, help me, and your eyes shall be half my masterpiece!' No one so loves and respects the rich realities of nature as the artist whose imagination caresses and flatters them. He knows what a fact may hold (whether Raphael knew, you may judge by his portrait, behind us there, of Tommaso Inghirami); bad his fancy hovers above it, as Ariel

17

hovered above the sleeping prince. There is only one Raphael, bad an artist may still be an artist. As I said last night, the days of illumination are gone; visions are rare; we have to look long to see them. But in meditation we may still cultivate the ideal; round it, smooth it, perfect it. The result—the result," (here his voice faltered suddenly, and he fixed his eyes for a moment on the picture; when they met my own again they were full of tears)—"the result may be less than this; but still it may be good, it may be *great!*" he cried with vehemence. "It may hang somewhere, in after years, in goodly company, and keep the artist's memory warm. Think of being known to mankind after some such fashion as this! of hanging here through the slow centuries in the gaze of an altered world; living on and on in the cunning of an eye and hand that are part of the dust of ages, a delight and a law to remote generations; making beauty a force and purity an example!"

"Heaven forbid," I said, smiling, "that I should take the wind out of your sails! But doesn't it occur to you that, besides being strong in his genius, Raphael was happy in a certain good faith of which we have lost the trick? There are people, I know, who deny that his spotless Madonnas are anything more than pretty blondes of that period enhanced by the Raphaelesque touch, which they declare is a profane touch. Be that as it may, people's religious and æsthetic needs went arm in arm, and there was, as I may say, a demand for the Blessed Virgin, visible and adorable, which must have given firmness to the artist's hand. I am afraid there is no demand now."

My companion seemed painfully puzzled; he shivered, as it were, in this chilling blast of scepticism. Then shaking his head with sublime confidence— "There is always a demand!" he cried; "that ineffable type is one of the eternal needs of man's heart; but pious souls long for it in silence, almost in shame. Let it appear, and their faith grows brave. How *should* it appear in this corrupt generation? It cannot be made to order. It could, indeed, when the order came, trumpet-toned, from the lips of the Church herself, and was addressed to genius panting with inspiration. But it can spring now only from the soil of passionate labour and culture. Do you really fancy that while, from time to time, a man of complete artistic vision is born into the world, that image can perish? The man who paints it has painted everything. The subject admits of every perfection—form, colour, expression, composition. It can be as simple as you please, and yet as rich; as broad and pure, and yet as full of delicate detail. Think of the chance for flesh in the little naked, nestling child, irradiating divinity; of the chance for drapery in the chaste and ample garment of the mother! think of the great story you compress into that simple theme! Think, above all, of the mother's face and its ineffable suggestiveness, of the mingled burden of joy and trouble, the tenderness turned to worship, and the worship turned to far-seeing pity! Then look at it all in perfect line and lovely colour, breathing truth and beauty and mastery!"

"Anch' io son pittore!" I cried. "Unless I am mistaken, you have a masterpiece on the stocks. If you put all that in, you will do more than Raphael himself did. Let me know when your picture is finished, and wherever in the wide world I may be, I will post back to Florence and pay my respects to—the *Madonna of the future!*"

He blushed vividly and gave a heavy sigh, half of protest, half of resignation. "I don't often mention my picture by name. I detest this modern custom of premature publicity. A great work needs silence, privacy, mystery even. And then, do you know, people are so cruel, so frivolous, so unable to imagine a man's wishing to paint a Madonna at this time of day, that I have been laughed at—laughed at, sir!" and his blush deepened to crimson. "I don't know what has prompted me to be so frank and trustful with you. You look as if you wouldn't laugh at me. My dear young man"—and he laid his hand on my arm—"I am worthy of respect. Whatever my talents may be, I am honest. There is nothing grotesque in a pure ambition, or in a life devoted to it."

There was something so sternly sincere in his look and tone that further questions seemed impertinent. I had repeated opportunity to ask them, however, for after this we spent much time together. Daily for a fortnight, we met by appointment, to see the sights. He knew the city so well, he had strolled and lounged so often through its streets and churches and galleries, he was so deeply versed in its greater and lesser memories, so imbued with the local genius, that he was an altogether ideal *valet de place*, and I was glad enough to leave my Murray at home, and gather facts and opinions alike from his gossiping commentary. He talked of Florence like a lover, and admitted that it was a very old affair; he had lost his heart to her at first sight. "It's the fashion to talk of all cities as feminine," he said, "but, as a rule, it's a monstrous mistake. Is Florence of the same sex as New York, as Chicago? She is the sole perfect lady of them all; one feels towards her as a lad in his teens feels to some beautiful older woman with a 'history.' She fills you with a sort of aspiring gallantry." This disinterested passion seemed to stand my friend in stead of the common social ties; he led a lonely life, and cared for nothing but his work. I was duly flattered by his having taken my frivolous self into his favour, and by his generous sacrifice of precious hours to my society. We spent many of these hours among those early paintings in which Florence is so rich, returning ever and anon, with restless sympathies, to wonder whether these tender blossoms of art had not a vital fragrance and savour more precious than the full-fruited knowledge of the later works. We lingered often in the sepulchral chapel of San Lorenzo, and watched Michael Angelo's dim-visaged warrior sitting there like some awful Genius of Doubt and brooding behind his eternal mask upon the mysteries of life. We stood more than once in the little convent chambers where Fra Angelico wrought as if an angel indeed had held his hand, and gathered that sense of scattered dews and early bird-notes which makes an hour among his relics seem like a morning stroll in some monkish garden. We did all this and much more—wandered into dark chapels, damp courts, and dusty palace-rooms, in quest of lingering hints of fresco and lurking treasures of carving.

I was more and more impressed with my companion's remarkable singleness of purpose. Everything was a pretext for some wildly idealistic rhapsody or reverie. Nothing could be seen or said that did not lead him sooner or later to a glowing discourse on the true, the beautiful, and the good. If my friend was not a genius, he was certainly a monomaniac; and I found as great a fascination in watching the odd lights and shades of his character as if he had been a creature from another planet. He seemed, indeed, to know very little of this one, and lived and moved altogether in his own little province of art. A creature more unsullied by the world it is impossible to conceive, and I often thought it a flaw in his artistic character that he had not a harmless vice or two. It amused me greatly at times to think that he was of our shrewd

Yankee race; but, after all, there could be no better token of his American origin than this high æsthetic fever. The very heat of his devotion was a sign of conversion; those born to European opportunity manage better to reconcile enthusiasm with comfort. He had, moreover, all our native mistrust for intellectual discretion, and our native relish for sonorous superlatives. As a critic he was very much more generous than just, and his mildest terms of approbation were "stupendous," "transcendent," and "incomparable." The small change of admiration seemed to him no coin for a gentleman to handle; and yet, frank as he was intellectually, he was personally altogether a mystery. His professions, somehow, were all half-professions, and his allusions to his work and circumstances left something dimly ambiguous in the background. He was modest and proud, and never spoke of his domestic matters. He was evidently poor; yet he must have had some slender independence, since he could afford to make so merry over the fact that his culture of ideal beauty had never brought him a penny. His poverty, I supposed, was his motive for neither inviting me to his lodging nor mentioning its whereabouts. We met either in some public place or at my hotel, where I entertained him as freely as I might without appearing to be prompted by charity. He seemed always hungry, and this was his nearest approach to human grossness. I made a point of asking no impertinent questions, but, each time we met, I ventured to make some respectful allusion to the *magnum opus*, to inquire, as it were, as to its health and progress. "We are getting on, with the Lord's help," he would say, with a grave smile. "We are doing well. You see, I have the grand advantage that I lose no time. These hours I spend with you are pure profit. They are *suggestive*! Just as the truly religious soul is always at worship, the genuine artist is always in labour. He takes his property wherever he finds it, and learns some precious secret from every object that stands up in the light. If you but knew the rapture of observation! I gather with every glance some hint for light, for colour, or relief! When I get home, I pour out my treasures into the lap of toy Madonna. Oh, I am not idle! *Nulla dies sine linea.*"

I was introduced in Florence to an American lady whose drawing-room had long formed an attractive place of reunion for the foreign residents. She lived on a fourth floor, and she was not rich; but she offered her visitors very good tea, little cakes at option, and conversation not quite to match. Her conversation had mainly an æsthetic flavour, for Mrs. Coventry was famously "artistic." Her apartment was a sort of Pitti Palace *au petit pied*. She possessed "early masters" by the dozen—a cluster of Peruginos in her dining-room, a Giotto in her boudoir, an Andrea del Sarto over her drawing-room chimney-piece. Surrounded by these treasures, and by innumerable bronzes, mosaics, majolica dishes, and little worm-eaten diptychs covered with angular saints on gilded backgrounds, our hostess enjoyed the dignity of a sort of high-priestess of the arts. She always wore on her bosom a huge miniature copy of the Madonna della Seggiola. Gaining her ear quietly one evening, I asked her whether she knew that remarkable man, Mr. Theobald.

"Know him!" she exclaimed; "know poor Theobald! All Florence knows him, his flame-coloured locks, his black velvet coat, his interminable harangues on the beautiful, and his wondrous Madonna that mortal eye has never seen, and that mortal patience has quite given up expecting."

"Really," I cried, "you don't believe in his Madonna?"

"My dear ingenuous youth," rejoined my shrewd friend, "has he made a convert of you? Well, we all believed in him once; he came down upon Florence and took the town by storm. Another Raphael, at the very least, had been born among men, and the poor dear United States were to have the credit of him. Hadn't he the very hair of Raphael flowing down on his shoulders? The hair, alas, but not the head! We swallowed him whole, however; we hung upon his lips and proclaimed his genius on the house-tops. The women were all dying to sit to him for their portraits and be made immortal, like Leonardo's Joconde. We decided that his manner was a good deal like Leonardo's—mysterious, and inscrutable, and fascinating. Mysterious it certainly was; mystery was the beginning and the end of it. The months passed by, and the miracle hung fire; our master never produced his masterpiece. He passed hours in the galleries and churches, posturing, musing, and gazing; he talked more than ever about the beautiful, but he never put brush to canvas. We had all subscribed, as it were, to the great performance; but as it never came off people began to ask for their money again. I was one of the last of the faithful; I carried devotion so far as to sit to him for my head. If you could have seen the horrible creature he made of me, you would admit that even a woman with no more vanity than will tie her bonnet straight must have cooled off then. The man didn't know the very alphabet of drawing! His strong point, he intimated, was his sentiment; but is it a consolation, when one has been painted a fright, to know it has been done with peculiar gusto? One by one, I confess, we fell away from the faith, and Mr. Theobald didn't lift his little finger to preserve us. At the first hint that we were tired of waiting, and that we should like the show to begin, he was off in a huff. 'Great work requires time, contemplation, privacy, mystery! O ye of little faith!' We answered that we didn't insist on a great work; that the five-act tragedy might come at his convenience; that we merely asked for something to keep us from yawning, some inexpensive little *lever de rideau*. Hereupon the poor man took his stand as a genius misconceived and persecuted, an *âme méconnue*, and washed his hands of us from that hour! No, I believe he does me the honour to consider me the head and front of the conspiracy formed to nip his glory in the bud—a bud that has taken twenty years to blossom. Ask him if he knows me, and he will tell you I am a horribly ugly old woman, who has vowed his destruction because he won't paint her portrait as a pendant to Titian's Flora. I fancy that since then he has had none but chance followers, innocent strangers like yourself, who have taken him at his word. The mountain is still in labour; I have not heard that the mouse has been born. I pass him once in a while in the galleries, and he fixes his great dark eyes on me with a sublimity of indifference, as if I were a bad copy of a Sassoferrato! It is a long time ago now that I heard that he was making studies for a Madonna who was to be a *résumé* of all the other Madonnas of the Italian school—like that antique Venus who borrowed a nose from one great image and an ankle from another. It's certainly a masterly idea. The parts may be fine, but when I think of my unhappy portrait I tremble for the whole. He has communicated this striking idea under the pledge of solemn secrecy to fifty chosen spirits, to every one he has ever been able to button-hole for five minutes. I suppose he wants to get an order for it, and he is not to blame; for Heaven knows how he lives. I see by your blush," my hostess frankly continued, "that you have been honoured with his confidence. You needn't be ashamed, my dear young man; a man of your age is none the worse for a certain generous credulity. Only allow me to give you a word of advice: keep your credulity out of your pockets! Don't pay for the picture till it's delivered. You have not been treated to a peep at it, I imagine! No more have your fifty predecessors in the faith. There are people who doubt whether there is any picture to be seen. I fancy, myself, that if one were to get into his studio, one would find something very like the picture in that tale of Balzac's—a mere mass of incoherent scratches and daubs, a jumble of dead paint!"

I listened to this pungent recital in silent wonder. It had a painfully plausible sound, and was not inconsistent with certain shy suspicions of my own. My hostess was not only a clever woman, but presumably a generous one. I determined to let my judgment wait upon events. Possibly she was right; but if she was wrong, she was cruelly wrong! Her version of my friend's eccentricities made me impatient to see him again and examine him in the light of public opinion. On our next meeting I immediately asked him if he knew Mrs. Coventry. He laid his hand on my arm and gave me a sad smile. "Has she taxed *your* gallantry at last?" he asked. "She's a foolish woman. She's frivolous and heartless, and she pretends to be serious and kind. She prattles about Giotto's second manner and Vittoria Colonna's liaison with 'Michael'— one would think that Michael lived across the way and was expected in to take a hand at whist—but she knows as little about art, and about the conditions of production, as I know about Buddhism. She profanes sacred words," he added more vehemently, after a pause. "She cares for you only as some one to band teacups in that horrible mendacious little parlour of hers, with its trumpery Peruginos! If you can't dash off a new picture every three days, and let her hand it round among her guests, she tells them in plain English that you are an impostor!"

This attempt of mine to test Mrs. Coventry's accuracy was made in the course of a late afternoon walk to the quiet old church of San Miniato, on one of the hill-tops which directly overlook the city, from whose gates you are guided to it by a stony and cypress-bordered walk, which seems a very fitting avenue to a shrine. No spot is more propitious to lingering repose than the broad terrace in front of the church, where, lounging against the parapet, you may glance in slow alternation from the black and yellow marbles of the church façade, seamed and cracked with time and wind-sown with a tender flora of its own, down to the full domes and slender towers of Florence and over to the blue sweep of the wide-mouthed cup of mountains into whose hollow the little treasure city has been dropped. I had proposed, as a diversion from the painful memories evoked by Mrs. Coventry's name, that Theobald should go with me the next evening to the opera, where some rarely-played work was to be given. He declined, as I half expected, for I observed that he regularly kept his evenings in reserve, and never alluded to his manner of passing them. "You have reminded me before," I said, smiling, "of that charming speech of the Florentine painter in Alfred de Musset's 'Lorenzaccio': 'I do no harm to anyone. I pass my days in my studio, On Sunday I go to the Annunziata or to Santa Mario; the monks think I have a voice; they dress me in a white gown and a red cap, and I take a share in the choruses; sometimes I do a little solo: these are the only times I go into public. In the evening, I visit my sweetheart; when the night is fine, we pass it on her balcony.' I don't know whether you have a sweetheart, or whether she has a balcony. But if you are so happy, it's certainly better than trying to find a charm in a third-rate prima donna."

He made no immediate response, but at last he turned to me solemnly. "Can you look upon a beautiful woman with reverent eyes?"

"Really," I said, "I don't pretend to be sheepish, but I should be sorry to think I was impudent." And I asked him what in the world he meant. When at last I had assured him that I could undertake to temper admiration with respect, he informed me, with an air of religious mystery, that it was in his power to introduce me to the most beautiful woman in Italy—"A beauty with a soul!"

"Upon my word," I cried, "you are extremely fortunate, and that is a most attractive description."

"This woman's beauty," he went on, "is a lesson, a morality, a poem! It's my daily study."

Of course, after this, I lost no time in reminding him of what, before we parted, had taken the shape of a promise. "I feel somehow," he had said, "as if it were a sort of violation of that privacy in which I have always contemplated her beauty. This is friendship, my friend. No hint of her existence has ever fallen from my lips. But with too great a familiarity we are apt to lose a sense of the real value of things, and you perhaps will throw some new light upon it and offer a fresher interpretation."

We went accordingly by appointment to a certain ancient house in the heart of Florence—the precinct of the Mercato Vecchio—and climbed a dark, steep staircase, to the very summit of the edifice. Theobald's beauty seemed as loftily exalted above the line of common vision as his artistic ideal was lifted above the usual practice of men. He passed without knocking into the dark vestibule of a small apartment, and, flinging open an inner door, ushered me into a small saloon. The room seemed mean and sombre, though I caught a glimpse of white curtains swaying gently at an open window. At a table, near a lamp, sat a woman dressed in black, working at a piece of embroidery. As Theobald entered she looked up calmly, with a smile; but seeing me she made a movement of surprise, and rose with a kind of stately grace. Theobald stepped forward, took her hand and kissed it, with an indescribable air of immemorial usage. As he bent his head she looked at me askance, and I thought she blushed.

"Behold the Serafina!" said Theobald, frankly, waving me forward. "This is a friend, and a lover of the arts," he added, introducing me. I received a smile, a curtsey, and a request to be seated.

The most beautiful woman in Italy was a person of a generous Italian type and of a great simplicity of demeanour. Seated again at her lamp, with her embroidery, she seemed to have nothing whatever to say. Theobald, bending towards her in a sort of Platonic ecstasy, asked her a dozen paternally tender questions as to her health, her state of mind, her occupations, and the progress of her embroidery, which he examined minutely and summoned me to admire. It was some portion of an ecclesiastical vestment—yellow satin wrought with an elaborate design of silver and gold. She made answer in a full rich voice, but with a brevity which I hesitated whether to attribute to native reserve or to the profane constraint of my presence. She had been that morning to confession; she had also been to market, and had bought a chicken for dinner. She felt very happy; she had nothing to complain of except that the people for whom she was making her vestment, and who furnished her materials, should be willing to put such rotten silver thread into the garment, as one might say, of the Lord. From time to time, as she took her slow stitches, she raised her eyes and covered me with a glance which seemed at first to denote a placid curiosity, but in which, as I saw it repeated, I thought I perceived the dim glimmer of an attempt to establish an understanding with me at the expense of our companion. Meanwhile, as mindful as possible of Theobald's injunction of reverence, I considered the lady's personal claims to the fine compliment he had paid her.

That she was indeed a beautiful woman I perceived, after recovering from the surprise of finding her without the freshness of youth. Her beauty was of a sort which, in losing youth, loses little of its essential charm, expressed for the most part as it was in form and structure, and, as Theobald would have said, in "composition." She was broad and ample, low-browed and large-eyed, dark and pale. Her thick brown hair hung low beside her cheek and ear, and seemed to drape her head with a covering as chaste and formal as the veil of a nun. The poise and carriage of her head were admirably free and noble, and they were the more effective that their freedom was at moments discreetly corrected by a little sanctimonious droop, which harmonised admirably with the level gaze of her dark and quiet eye. A strong, serene, physical nature, and the placid temper which comes of no nerves and no troubles, seemed this lady's comfortable portion. She was dressed in plain dull black, save for a sort of dark blue kerchief which was folded across her bosom and exposed a glimpse of her massive throat. Over this kerchief was suspended a little silver cross. I admired her greatly, and yet with a large reserve. A certain mild intellectual apathy belonged properly to her type of beauty, and had always seemed to round and enrich it; but this *bourgeoise* Egeria, if I viewed her right, betrayed a rather vulgar stagnation of mind. There might have been once a dim spiritual light in her face; but it had long since begun to wane. And furthermore, in plain prose, she was growing stout. My disappointment amounted very nearly to complete disenchantment when Theobald, as if to facilitate my covert inspection, declaring that the lamp was very dim, and that she would ruin her eyes without more light, rose and fetched a couple of candles from the mantelpiece, which he placed lighted on the table. In this brighter illumination I perceived that our hostess was decidedly an elderly woman. She was neither haggard, nor worn, nor gray; she was simply coarse. The "soul" which Theobald had promised seemed scarcely worth making such a point of; it was no deeper mystery than a sort of matronly mildness of lip and brow. I should have been ready even to declare that that sanctified bend of the head was nothing more than the trick of a person constantly working at embroidery. It occurred to me even that it was a trick of a less innocent sort; for, in spite of the mellow quietude of her wits, this stately needlewoman dropped a hint that she took the situation rather less seriously than her friend. When he rose to light the candles she looked across at me with a quick, intelligent smile, and tapped her forehead with her forefinger; then, as from a sudden feeling of compassionate loyalty to poor Theobald, I preserved a blank face, she gave a little shrug and resumed her work.

What was the relation of this singular couple? Was he the most ardent of friends or the most reverent of lovers? Did she regard him as an eccentric swain, whose benevolent admiration of her beauty she was not ill pleased to humour at this small cost of having him climb into her little parlour and gossip of summer nights? With her decent and sombre dress, her simple gravity, and that fine piece of priestly needlework, she looked like some pious lay-member of a sisterhood, living by special permission outside her convent walls. Or was she maintained here aloft by her friend in comfortable leisure, so that he might have before him the perfect, eternal type, uncorrupted and untarnished by the struggle for existence? Her shapely hands, I observed, wore very fair and white; they lacked the traces of what is called honest toil.

"And the pictures, how do they come on?" she asked of Theobald, after a long pause.

"Finely, finely! I have here a friend whose sympathy and encouragement give me new faith and ardour."

Our hostess turned to me, gazed at me a moment rather inscrutably, and then tapping her forehead with the gesture she had used a minute before, "He has a magnificent genius!" she said, with perfect gravity.

"I am inclined to think so," I answered, with a smile.

"Eh, why do you smile?" she cried. "If you doubt it, you must see the *bambino*!" And she took the lamp and conducted me to the other side of the room, where on the wall, in a plain black frame, hung a large drawing in red chalk. Beneath it was fastened a little howl for holy water. The drawing represented a very young child, entirely naked, half nestling back against his mother's gown, but with his two little arms outstretched, as if in the act of benediction. It was executed with singular freedom and power, and yet seemed vivid with the sacred bloom of infancy. A sort of dimpled elegance and grace, mingled with its boldness, recalled the touch of Correggio. "That's what he can do!" said my hostess. "It's the blessed little boy whom I lost. It's his very image, and the Signor Teobaldo gave it me as a gift. He has given me many things besides!"

I looked at the picture for some time and admired it immensely. Turning back to Theobald I assured him that if it were hung among the drawings in the Uffizi and labelled with a glorious name it would hold its own. My praise seemed to give him extreme pleasure; he pressed my hands, and his eyes filled with tears. It moved him apparently with the desire to expatiate on the history of the drawing, for he rose and made his adieux to our companion, kissing her band with the same mild ardour as before. It occurred to me that the offer of a similar piece of gallantry on my own part might help me to know what manner of woman she was. When she perceived my intention she withdrew her hand, dropped her eyes solemnly, and made me a severe curtsey. Theobald took my arm and led me rapidly into the street.

"And what do you think of the divine Serafina?" he cried with fervour.

"It is certainly an excellent style of good looks!" I answered.

He eyed me an instant askance, and then seemed hurried along by the current of remembrance. "You should have seen the mother and the child together, seen them as I first saw them—the mother with her head draped in a shawl, a divine trouble in her face, and the bambino pressed to her bosom. You would have said, I think, that Raphael had found his match in common chance. I was coming in, one summer night, from a long walk in the country, when I met this apparition at the city gate. The woman held out her hand. I hardly knew whether to say, 'What do you want?' or to fall down and worship. She asked for a little money. I saw that she was beautiful and pale; she might have stepped out of the stable of Bethlehem! I gave her money and helped her on her way into the town. I had guessed her story. She, too, was a maiden mother, and she had been turned out into the world in her shame. I felt in all my pulses that here was my subject marvellously realised. I felt like one of the old monkish artists who had had a vision. I rescued the poor creatures, cherished them, watched them as I would have done some precious work of art, some lovely fragment of fresco discovered in a mouldering cloister. In a month—as if to deepen and sanctify the sadness and sweetness of it all—the poor little child died. When she felt that he was going she held him up to me for ten minutes, and I made that sketch. You saw a feverish haste in it, I suppose; I wanted to spare the poor little mortal the pain of his position. After that I doubly valued the mother. She is the simplest, sweetest, most natural creature that ever bloomed in this brave old land of Italy. She lives in the memory of her child, in her gratitude for the scanty kindness I have been able to show her, and in her simple religion! She is not even conscious of her beauty; my admiration has never made her vain. Heaven knows that I have made no secret of it. You must have observed the singular transparency of her expression, the lovely modesty of her glance. And was there ever such a truly virginal brow, such a natural classic elegance in the wave of the hair and the arch of the forehead? I have studied her; I may say I know her. I have absorbed her little by little; my mind is stamped and imbued, and I have determined now to clinch the impression; I shall at last invite her to sit for me!"

"'At last—at last'?" I repeated, in much amazement. "Do you mean that she has never done so yet?"

"I have not really had—a—a sitting," said Theobald, speaking very slowly. "I have taken notes, you know; I have got my grand fundamental impression. That's the great thing! But I have not actually had her as a model, posed and draped and lighted, before my easel."

30

What had become for the moment of my perception and my tact I am at a loss to say; in their absence I was unable to repress a headlong exclamation. I was destined to regret it. We had stopped at a turning, beneath a lamp. "My poor friend," I exclaimed, laying my hand on his shoulder, "you have *dawdled*! She's an old, old woman—for a Madonna!"

It was as if I had brutally struck him; I shall never forget the long, slow, almost ghastly look of pain, with which he answered me.

"Dawdled?—old, old?" he stammered. "Are you joking?"

"Why, my dear fellow, I suppose you don't take her for a woman of twenty?"

He drew a long breath and leaned against a house, looking at me with questioning, protesting, reproachful eyes. At last, starting forward, and grasping my arm—"Answer me solemnly: does she seem to you truly old? Is she wrinkled, is she faded, am I blind?"

Then at last I understood the immensity of his illusion how, one by one, the noiseless years had ebbed away and left him brooding in charmed inaction, for ever preparing for a work for ever deferred. It seemed to me almost a kindness now to tell him the plain truth. "I should be sorry to say you are blind," I answered, "but I think you are deceived. You have lost time in effortless contemplation. Your friend was once young and fresh and virginal; but, I protest, that was some years ago. Still, she has *de beaux restes*. By all means make her sit for you!" I broke down; his face was too horribly reproachful.

He took off his hat and stood passing his handkerchief mechanically over his forehead. "*De beaux restes*? I thank you for sparing me the plain English. I must make up my Madonna out of *de beaux restes*! What a masterpiece she will be! Old—old! Old—old!" he murmured.

"Never mind her age," I cried, revolted at what I had done, "never mind my impression of her! You have your memory, your notes, your genius. Finish your picture in a month. I pronounce it beforehand a masterpiece, and I hereby offer you for it any sum you may choose to ask."

He stared, but he seemed scarcely to understand me. "Old—old!" he kept stupidly repeating. "If she is old, what am I? If her beauty has faded, where—where is my strength? Has life been a dream? Have I worshipped too long—have I loved too well?" The charm, in truth, was broken. That the chord of illusion should have snapped at my light accidental touch showed how it had been weakened by excessive tension. The poor fellow's sense of wasted time, of vanished opportunity, seemed to roll in upon his soul in waves of darkness. He suddenly dropped his head and burst into tears.

I led him homeward with all possible tenderness, but I attempted neither to check his grief, to restore his equanimity, nor to unsay the hard truth. When we reached my hotel I tried to induce him to come so.

"We will drink a glass of wine," I said, smiling, "to the completion of the Madonna."

With a violent effort he held up his head, mused for a moment with a formidably sombre frown, and then giving me his hand, "I will finish it," he cried, "in a month! No, in a fortnight! After all, I have it *here*!" And he tapped his forehead. "Of course she's old! She can afford to have it said of her—a woman who has made twenty years pass like a twelvemonth! Old—old! Why, sir, she shall be eternal!"

I wished to see him safely to his own door, but he waved me back and walked away with an air of resolution, whistling and swinging his cane. I waited a moment, and then followed him at a distance, and saw him proceed to cross the Santa Trinità Bridge. When he reached the middle he suddenly paused, as if his strength had deserted him, and leaned upon the parapet gazing over into the river. I was careful to keep him in sight; I confess that I passed ten very nervous minutes. He recovered himself at last, and went his way, slowly and with hanging head.

That I had really startled poor Theobald into a bolder use of his long-garnered stores of knowledge and taste, into the vulgar effort and hazard of production, seemed at first reason enough for his continued silence and absence; but as day followed day without his either calling or sending me a line, and without my meeting him in his customary haunts, in the galleries, in the Chapel at San Lorenzo, or strolling between the Arno side and the great hedge-screen of verdure which, along the drive of the Cascine, throws the fair occupants of barouche and phaeton into such becoming relief—as for more than a week I got neither tidings nor sight of him, I began to fear that I had fatally offended him, and that, instead of giving a wholesome impetus to his talent, I had brutally paralysed it. I had a wretched suspicion that I had made him ill. My stay at Florence was drawing to a close, and it was important that, before resuming my journey, I should assure myself of the truth. Theobald, to the last, had kept his lodging a mystery, and I was altogether at a loss where to look for him. The simplest course was to make inquiry of the beauty of the Mercato Vecchio, and I confess that unsatisfied curiosity as to the lady herself counselled it as well. Perhaps I had done her injustice, and she was as immortally fresh and fair as be conceived her. I was, at any rate, anxious to behold once more the ripe enchantress who had made twenty years pass as a twelvemonth. I repaired accordingly, one morning, to her abode, climbed the interminable staircase, and reached her door. It stood ajar, and as I hesitated whether to enter, a little serving-maid came clattering out with an empty kettle, as if she had just performed some savoury errand. The inner door, too, was open; so I crossed the little vestibule and entered the room in which I had formerly been received. It had not its evening aspect. The table, or one end of it, was spread for a late breakfast, and before it sat a gentleman—an individual, at least, of the male sex—doing execution upon a beefsteak and onions, and a bottle of wine. At his elbow, in friendly proximity, was placed the lady of the house. Her attitude, as I entered, was not that of an enchantress. With one hand she held in her lap a plate of smoking maccaroni; with the other she had lifted high in air one of the pendulous filaments of this succulent compound, and was in the act of slipping it gently down her throat. On the uncovered end of the table, facing her companion, were ranged half a dozen small statuettes, of some snuff-coloured substance resembling terra-cotta. He, brandishing his knife with ardour, was apparently descanting on their merits.

Evidently I darkened the door. My hostess dropped liner maccaroni—into her mouth, and rose hastily with a harsh exclamation and a flushed face. I immediately perceived that the Signora Serafina's secret was even better worth knowing than I had supposed, and that the way to learn it was to take it for granted. I summoned my best Italian, I smiled and bowed and apologised for my intrusion; and in a moment, whether or no I had dispelled the lady's irritation, I had at least stimulated her prudence. I was welcome, she said; I must take a seat. This was another friend of hers—also an artist, she declared with a smile which was almost amiable. Her companion wiped his moustache and bowed with great civility. I saw at a glance that he was equal to the situation. He was presumably the author of the statuettes on the table, and he knew a money-spending *forestiére* when he saw one. He was a small wiry man, with a clever, impudent, tossed-up nose, a sharp little black eye, and waxed ends to his moustache. On the side of his head he wore jauntily a little crimson velvet smoking-cap, and I observed that his feet were encased in brilliant slippers. On Serafina's remarking with dignity that I was the friend of Mr. Theobald, he broke out into that fantastic French of which certain Italians are so insistently lavish, and declared with fervour that Mr. Theobald was a magnificent genius.

"I am sure I don't know," I answered with a shrug. "If you are in a position to affirm it, you have the advantage of me. I have seen nothing from his hand but the bambino yonder, which certainly is fine."

He declared that the bambino was a masterpiece, a pure Corregio. It was only a pity, he added with a knowing laugh, that the sketch had not been made on some good bit of honeycombed old panel. The stately Serafina hereupon protested that Mr. Theobald was the soul of honour, and that he would never lend himself to a deceit. "I am not a judge of genius," she said, "and I know nothing of pictures. I am but a poor simple widow; but I know that the Signor Teobaldo has the heart of an angel and the virtue of a saint. He is my benefactor," she added sententiously. The after-glow of the somewhat sinister flush with which she had greeted me still lingered in her cheek, and perhaps did not favour her beauty; I could not but fancy it a wise custom of Theobald's to visit her only by candle-light. She was coarse, and her pour adorer was a poet.

"I have the greatest esteem for him," I said; "it is for this reason that I have been uneasy at not seeing him for ten days. Have you seen him? Is he perhaps ill?"

"Ill! Heaven forbid!" cried Serafina, with genuine vehemence.

Her companion uttered a rapid expletive, and reproached her with not having been to see him. She hesitated a moment; then she simpered the least bit and bridled. "He comes to see me—without reproach! But it would not be the same for me to go to him, though, indeed, you may almost call him a man of holy life."

"He has the greatest admiration for you," I said. "He would have been honoured by your visit."

She looked at me a moment sharply. "More admiration than you. Admit that!" Of course I protested with all the eloquence at my command, and my mysterious hostess then confessed that she had taken no fancy to me on my former visit, and that, Theobald not having returned, she believed I had poisoned his mind against her. "It would be no kindness to the poor gentleman, I can tell you that," she said. "He has come to see me every evening for years. It's a long friendship! No one knows him as well as I."

"I don't pretend to know him or to understand him," I said. "He's a mystery! Nevertheless, he seems to me a little—" And I touched my forehead and waved my hand in the air.

Serafina glanced at her companion a moment, as if for inspiration. He contented himself with shrugging his shoulders as he filled his glass again. The *padrona* hereupon gave me a more softly insinuating smile than would have seemed likely to bloom on so candid a brow. "It's for that that I love him!" she said. "The world has so little kindness for such persons. It laughs at them, and despises them, and cheats them. He is too good for this wicked life! It's his fancy that he finds a little Paradise up here in my poor apartment. If he thinks so, how can I help it? He has a strange belief—really, I ought to be ashamed to tell you—that I resemble the Blessed Virgin: Heaven forgive me! I let him think what he pleases, so long as it makes him happy. He was very kind to me once, and I am not one that forgets a favour. So I receive him every evening civilly, and ask after his health, and let him look at me on this side and that! For that matter, I may say it without vanity, I was worth looking at once! And he's not always amusing, poor man! He sits sometimes for an hour without speaking a word, or else he talks away, without stopping, on art and nature, and beauty and duty, and fifty fine things that are all so much Latin to me. I beg you to understand that he has never said a word to me that I mightn't decently listen to. He may be a little cracked, but he's one of the blessed saints."

"Eh!" cried the man, "the blessed saints were all a little cracked!"

Serafina, I fancied, left part of her story untold; but she told enough of it to make poor Theobald's own statement seem intensely pathetic in its exalted simplicity. "It's a strange fortune, certainly," she went on, "to have such a friend as this dear man—a friend who is less than a lover and more than a friend." I glanced at her companion, who preserved an impenetrable smile, twisted the end of his moustache, and disposed of a copious mouthful. Was *he* less than a lover? "But what will you have?" Serafina pursued. "In this hard world one must not ask too many questions; one must take what comes and keep what one gets. I have kept my good friend for twenty years, and I do hope that, at this time of day, signore, you have not come to turn him against me!"

I assured her that I had no such design, and that I should vastly regret disturbing Mr. Theobald's habits or convictions. On the contrary, I was alarmed about him, and I should immediately go in search of him. She gave me his address, and a florid account of her sufferings at his non-appearance. She had not been to him for various reasons; chiefly because she was afraid of displeasing him, as he had always made such a mystery of his home. "You might have sent this gentleman!" I ventured to suggest.

"Ah," cried the gentleman, "he admires the Signora Serafina, but he wouldn't admire me." And then, confidentially, with his finger on his nose, "He's a purist!"

I was about to withdraw, after having promised that I would inform the Signora Serafina of my friend's condition, when her companion, who had risen from table and girded his loins apparently for the onset, grasped me gently by the arm, and led me before the row of statuettes. "I perceive by your conversation, signore, that you are a patron of the arts. Allow me

36

to request your honourable attention for these modest products of my own ingenuity. They are brand-new, fresh from my atelier, and have never been exhibited in public. I have brought them here to receive the verdict of this dear lady, who is a good critic, for all she may pretend to the contrary. I am the inventor of this peculiar style of statuette—of subject, manner, material, everything. Touch them, I pray you; handle them freely—you needn't fear. Delicate as they look, it is impossible they should break! My various creations have met with great success. They are especially admired by Americans. I have sent them all over Europe—to London, Paris, Vienna! You may have observed some little specimens in Paris, on the Boulevard, in a shop of which they constitute the specialty. There is always a crowd about the window. They form a very pleasing ornament for the mantel-shelf of a gay young bachelor, for the boudoir of a pretty woman. You couldn't make a prettier present to a person with whom you wished to exchange a harmless joke. It is not classic art, signore, of course; but, between ourselves, isn't classic art sometimes rather a bore? Caricature, burlesque, *la charge*, as the French say, has hitherto been confined to paper, to the pen and pencil. Now, it has been my inspiration to introduce it into statuary. For this purpose I have invented a peculiar plastic compound which you will permit me not to divulge. That's my secret, signore! It's as light, you perceive, as cork, and yet as firm as alabaster! I frankly confess that I really pride myself as much on this little stroke of chemical ingenuity as upon the other element of novelty in my creations—my types. What do you say to my types, signore? The idea is bold; does it strike you as happy? Cats and monkeys—monkeys and cats—all human life is there! Human life, of course, I mean, viewed with the eye of the satirist! To combine sculpture and satire, signore, has been my unprecedented ambition. I flatter myself that I have not egregiously failed."

As this jaunty Juvenal of the chimney-piece delivered himself of his persuasive allocution, he took up his little groups successively from the table, held them aloft, turned them about, rapped them with his knuckles, and gazed at them lovingly, with his head on one side. They consisted each of a cat and a monkey, fantastically draped, in some preposterously sentimental conjunction. They exhibited a certain sameness of motive, and illustrated chiefly the different phases of what, in delicate terms, may be called gallantry

37

and coquetry; but they were strikingly clever and expressive, and were at once very perfect cats and monkeys and very natural men and women. I confess, however, that they failed to amuse me. I was doubtless not in a mood to enjoy them, for they seemed to me peculiarly cynical and vulgar. Their imitative felicity was revolting. As I looked askance at the complacent little artist, brandishing them between finger and thumb and caressing them with an amorous eye, he seemed to me himself little more than an exceptionally intelligent ape. I mustered an admiring grin, however, and he blew another blast. "My figures are studied from life! I have a little menagerie of monkeys whose frolics I contemplate by the hour. As for the cats, one has only to look out of one's back window! Since I have begun to examine these expressive little brutes, I have made many profound observations. Speaking, signore, to a man of imagination, I may say that my little designs are not without a philosophy of their own. Truly, I don't know whether the cats and monkeys imitate us, or whether it's we who imitate them." I congratulated him on his philosophy, and he resumed: "You will do use the honour to admit that I have handled my subjects with delicacy. Eh, it was needed, signore! I have been free, but not too free—eh? Just a hint, you know! You may see as much or as little as you please. These little groups, however, are no measure of my invention. If you will favour me with a call at my studio, I think that you will admit that my combinations are really infinite. I likewise execute figures to command. You have perhaps some little motive—the fruit of your philosophy of life, signore—which you would like to have interpreted. I can promise to work it up to your satisfaction; it shall be as malicious as you please! Allow me to present you with my card, and to remind you that my prices are moderate. Only sixty francs for a little group like that. My statuettes are as durable as bronze—*ære perennius*, signore—and, between ourselves, I think they are more amusing!"

As I pocketed his card I glanced at Madonna Serafina, wondering whether she had an eye for contrasts. She had picked up one of the little couples and was tenderly dusting it with a feather broom.

What I had just seen and heard had so deepened my compassionate interest in my deluded friend that I took a summary leave, making my way directly to the house designated by this remarkable woman. It was in an obscure corner of the opposite side of the town, and presented a sombre and squalid appearance. An old woman in the doorway, on my inquiring for Theobald, ushered me in with a mumbled blessing and an expression of relief at the poor gentleman having a friend. His lodging seemed to consist of a single room at the top of the house. On getting no answer to my knock, I opened the door, supposing that he was absent, so that it gave me a certain shock to find him sitting there helpless and dumb. He was seated near the single window, facing an easel which supported a large canvas. On my entering he looked up at me blankly, without changing his position, which was that of absolute lassitude and dejection, his arms loosely folded, his legs stretched before him, his head hanging on his breast. Advancing into the room I perceived that his face vividly corresponded with his attitude. He was pale, haggard, and unshaven, and his dull and sunken eye gazed at me without a spark of recognition. I had been afraid that he would greet me with fierce reproaches, as the cruelly officious patron who had turned his contentment to bitterness, and I was relieved to find that my appearance awakened no visible resentment. "Don't you know me?" I asked, as I put out my hand. "Have you already forgotten me?"

He made no response, kept his position stupidly, and left me staring about the room. It spoke most plaintively for itself. Shabby, sordid, naked, it contained, beyond the wretched bed, but the scantiest provision for personal comfort. It was bedroom at once and studio—a grim ghost of a studio. A few dusty casts and prints on the walls, three or four old canvases turned face inward, and a rusty-looking colour-box, formed, with the easel at the window, the sum of its appurtenances. The place savoured horribly of poverty. Its only wealth was the picture on the easel, presumably the famous Madonna. Averted as this was from the door, I was unable to see its face; but at last, sickened by the vacant misery of the spot, I passed behind Theobald, eagerly and tenderly. I can hardly say that I was surprised at what I found—a canvas that was a mere dead blank, cracked and discoloured by time. This was his immortal work! Though not surprised, I confess I was powerfully moved, and I think that for five minutes I could not have trusted myself to speak. At last my silent nearness affected him; he stirred and turned, and then rose and looked at me with a slowly kindling eye. I murmured some kind ineffective nothings about his being ill and needing advice and care, but he seemed absorbed in the effort to recall distinctly what had last passed between us. "You were right," he said, with a pitiful smile, "I am a dawdler! I am a failure! I shall do nothing more in this world. You opened my eyes; and, though the truth is bitter, I bear you no grudge. Amen! I have been sitting here for a week, face to face with the truth, with the past, with my weakness and poverty and nullity. I shall never touch a brush! I believe I have neither eaten nor slept. Look at that canvas!" he went on, as I relieved my emotion in an urgent request that he would come home with me and dine. "That was to have contained my masterpiece! Isn't it a promising foundation? The elements of it are all *here*." And he tapped his forehead with that mystic confidence which had marked the gesture before. "If I could only transpose them into some brain that has the hand, the will! Since I have been sitting here taking stock of my intellects, I have come to believe that I have the material for a hundred masterpieces. But my hand is paralysed now, and they will never be painted. I never began! I waited and waited to be worthier to begin, and wasted my life in preparation. While I fancied my creation was growing it was dying. I have taken it all too hard! Michael Angelo didn't, when he went at the Lorenzo! He did his best at a venture, and his venture is immortal. *That's* mine!" And he pointed with a gesture I shall never forget at the empty canvas. "I suppose we are a genus by ourselves in the providential scheme—we talents that can't act, that can't do nor dare! We take it out in talk, in plans and promises, in study, in visions! But our visions, let me tell you," he cried, with a toss of his head, "have a way of being brilliant, and a man has not lived in vain who has seen the things I have seen! Of course you will not believe in them when that bit of worm-eaten cloth is all I have to show for them; but to convince you, to enchant and astound the world, I need only the hand of Raphael. His brain I already have. A pity, you will say, that I haven't his modesty! Ah, let me boast and babble now; it's all I have left! I am the half of a genius! Where in the wide world is my other half? Lodged perhaps in the vulgar soul, the cunning, ready fingers of some dull copyist or some trivial artisan, who turns out by the dozen his easy prodigies of touch! But it's not for me to sneer at him; he at least does something. He's not a dawdler! Well for me if I had been vulgar and clever and reckless, if I could have shut my eyes and taken my leap."

What to say to the poor fellow, what to do for him, seemed hard to determine; I chiefly felt that I must break the spell of his present inaction, and remove him from the haunted atmosphere of the little room it was such a cruel irony to call a studio. I cannot say I persuaded him to come out with me; he simply suffered himself to be led, and when we began to walk in the open air I was able to appreciate his pitifully weakened condition. Nevertheless, he seemed in a certain way to revive, and murmured at last that he should like to go to the Pitti Gallery. I shall never forget our melancholy stroll through those gorgeous halls, every picture on whose walls seemed, even to my own sympathetic vision, to glow with a sort of insolent renewal of strength and lustre. The eyes and lips of the great portraits appeared to smile in ineffable scorn of the dejected pretender who had dreamed of competing with their triumphant authors; the celestial candour, even, of the Madonna of the Chair, as we paused in perfect silence before her, was tinged with the sinister irony of the women of Leonardo. Perfect silence, indeed, marked our whole progress—the silence of a deep farewell; for I felt in all my pulses, as Theobald, leaning on my arm, dragged one heavy foot after the other, that he was looking his last. When we came out he was so exhausted that instead of taking him to my hotel to dine, I called a carriage and drove him straight to his own poor lodging. He had sunk into an extraordinary lethargy; he lay back in the carriage, with his eyes closed, as pale as death, his faint breathing interrupted at intervals by a sudden gasp, like a smothered sob or a vain attempt to speak. With the help of the old woman who had admitted me before, and who emerged from a dark back court, I contrived to lead him up the long steep staircase and lay him on his wretched bed. To her I gave him in charge, while I prepared in all haste to seek a physician. But she followed me out of the room with a pitiful clasping of her hands.

"Poor, dear, blessed gentleman," she murmured; "is he dying?"

"Possibly. How long has he been thus?"

"Since a certain night he passed ten days ago. I came up in the morning to make his poor bed, and found him sitting up in his clothes before that great canvas he keeps there. Poor, dear, strange man, he says his prayers to it! He had not been to bed, nor since then, properly! What has happened to him? Has he found out about the Serafina?" she whispered, with a glittering eye and a toothless grin.

"Prove at least that one old woman can be faithful," I said, "and watch him well till I come back." My return was delayed, through the absence of the English physician, who was away on a round of visits, and whom I vainly pursued from house to house before I overtook him. I brought him to Theobald's bedside none too soon. A violent fever had seized our patient, and the case was evidently grave. A couple of hours later I knew that he had brain fever. From this moment I was with him constantly; but I am far from wishing to describe his illness. Excessively painful to witness, it was happily brief. Life burned out in delirium. One night in particular that I passed at his pillow, listening to his wild snatches of regret, of aspiration, of rapture and awe at the phantasmal pictures with which his brain seemed to swarm, comes back to my memory now like some stray page from a lost masterpiece of tragedy. Before a week was over we had buried him in the little Protestant cemetery on the way to Fiesole. The Signora Serafina, whom I had caused to be informed of his illness, had come in person, I was told, to inquire about its progress; but she was absent from his funeral, which was attended by but a scanty concourse of mourners. Half a dozen old Florentine sojourners, in spite of the prolonged estrangement which had preceded his death, had felt the kindly impulse to honour his grave. Among them was my friend Mrs. Coventry, whom I found, on my departure, waiting in her carriage at the gate of the cemetery.

"Well," she said, relieving at last with a significant smile the solemnity of our immediate greeting, "and the great Madonna? Have you seen her, after all?"

"I have seen her," I said; "she is mine—by bequest. But I shall never show her to you."

"And why not, pray?"

"My dear Mrs. Coventry, you would not understand her!"

"Upon my word, you are polite."

"Excuse me; I am sad and vexed and bitter." And with reprehensible rudeness I marched away. I was excessively impatient to leave Florence; my friend's dark spirit seemed diffused through all things. I had packed my trunk to start for Rome that night, and meanwhile, to beguile my unrest, I aimlessly paced the streets. Chance led me at last to the church of San Lorenzo. Remembering poor Theobald's phrase about Michael Angelo—"He did his best at a venture"—I went in and turned my steps to the chapel of the tombs. Viewing in sadness the sadness of its immortal treasures, I fancied, while I stood there, that they needed no ampler commentary than these simple words. As I passed through the church again to leave it, a woman, turning away from one of the side altars, met me face to face. The black shawl depending from her head draped picturesquely the handsome visage of Madonna Serafina. She stopped as she recognised me, and I saw that she wished to speak. Her eye was bright, and her ample bosom heaved in a way that seemed to portend a certain sharpness of reproach. But the expression of my own face, apparently, drew the sting from her resentment, and she addressed me in a tone in which bitterness was tempered by a sort of dogged resignation. "I know it was you, now, that separated us," she said. "It was a pity he ever brought you to see me! Of course, you couldn't think of me as he did. Well, the Lord gave him, the Lord has taken him. I have just paid for a nine days' mass for his soul. And I can tell you this, signore—I never deceived him. Who put it into his head that I was made to live on holy thoughts and fine phrases? It was his own fancy, and it pleased him to think so.—Did he suffer much?" she added more softly, after a pause.

"His sufferings were great, but they were short."

"And did he speak of me?" She had hesitated and dropped her eyes; she raised them with her question, and revealed in their sombre stillness a gleam of feminine confidence which, for the moment, revived and illumined her beauty. Poor Theobald! Whatever name he had given his passion, it was still her fine eyes that had charmed him.

"Be contented, madam," I answered, gravely.

She dropped her eyes again and was silent. Then exhaling a full rich sigh, as she gathered her shawl together—"He was a magnificent genius!"

I bowed, and we separated.

Passing through a narrow side street on my way back to my hotel, I perceived above a doorway a sign which it seemed to me I had read before. I suddenly remembered that it was identical with the superscription of a card that I had carried for an hour in my waistcoat pocket. On the threshold stood the ingenious artist whose claims to public favour were thus distinctly signalised, smoking a pipe in the evening air, and giving the finishing polish with a bit of rag to one of his inimitable "combinations." I caught the expressive curl of a couple of tails. He recognised me, removed his little red cap with a most obsequious bow, and motioned me to enter his studio. I returned his salute and passed on, vexed with the apparition. For a week afterwards, whenever I was seized among the ruins of triumphant Rome with some peculiarly poignant memory of Theobald's transcendent illusions and deplorable failure, I seemed to hear a fantastic, impertinent murmur, "Cats and monkeys, monkeys and cats; all human life there!"

About Author

Henry James OM (15 April 1843 – 28 February 1916) was an American-British author regarded as a key transitional figure between literary realism and literary modernism, and is considered by many to be among the greatest novelists in the English language. He was the son of Henry James Sr. and the brother of renowned philosopher and psychologist William James and diarist Alice James.

He is best known for a number of novels dealing with the social and marital interplay between émigré Americans, English people, and continental Europeans. Examples of such novels include The Portrait of a Lady, The Ambassadors, and The Wings of the Dove. His later works were increasingly experimental. In describing the internal states of mind and social dynamics of his characters, James often made use of a style in which ambiguous or contradictory motives and impressions were overlaid or juxtaposed in the discussion of a character's psyche. For their unique ambiguity, as well as for other aspects of their composition, his late works have been compared to impressionist painting.

His novella The Turn of the Screw has garnered a reputation as the most analysed and ambiguous ghost story in the English language and remains his most widely adapted work in other media. He also wrote a number of other highly regarded ghost stories and is considered one of the greatest masters of the field.

James published articles and books of criticism, travel, biography, autobiography, and plays. Born in the United States, James largely relocated to Europe as a young man and eventually settled in England, becoming a British subject in 1915, one year before his death. James was nominated for the Nobel Prize in Literature in 1911, 1912 and 1916.

Life

Early years, 1843–1883

James was born at 2 Washington Place in New York City on 15 April 1843. His parents were Mary Walsh and Henry James Sr. His father was intelligent and steadfastly congenial. He was a lecturer and philosopher who had inherited independent means from his father, an Albany banker and investor. Mary came from a wealthy family long settled in New York City. Her sister Katherine lived with her adult family for an extended period of time. Henry Jr. had three brothers, William, who was one year his senior, and younger brothers Wilkinson (Wilkie) and Robertson. His younger sister was Alice. Both of his parents were of Irish and Scottish descent.

The family first lived in Albany, at 70 N. Pearl St., and then moved to Fourteenth Street in New York City when James was still a young boy. His education was calculated by his father to expose him to many influences, primarily scientific and philosophical; it was described by Percy Lubbock, the editor of his selected letters, as "extraordinarily haphazard and promiscuous." James did not share the usual education in Latin and Greek classics. Between 1855 and 1860, the James' household traveled to London, Paris, Geneva, Boulogne-sur-Mer and Newport, Rhode Island, according to the father's current interests and publishing ventures, retreating to the United States when funds were low. Henry studied primarily with tutors and briefly attended schools while the family traveled in Europe. Their longest stays were in France, where Henry began to feel at home and became fluent in French. He was afflicted with a stutter, which seems to have manifested itself only when he spoke English; in French, he did not stutter.

In 1860 the family returned to Newport. There Henry became a friend of the painter John La Farge, who introduced him to French literature, and in particular, to Balzac. James later called Balzac his "greatest master," and said that he had learned more about the craft of fiction from him than from anyone else.

In the autumn of 1861 Henry received an injury, probably to his back, while fighting a fire. This injury, which resurfaced at times throughout his life, made him unfit for military service in the American Civil War.

In 1864 the James family moved to Boston, Massachusetts to be near William, who had enrolled first in the Lawrence Scientific School at Harvard and then in the medical school. In 1862 Henry attended Harvard Law School, but realised that he was not interested in studying law. He pursued his interest in literature and associated with authors and critics William Dean Howells and Charles Eliot Norton in Boston and Cambridge, formed lifelong friendships with Oliver Wendell Holmes Jr., the future Supreme Court Justice, and with James and Annie Fields, his first professional mentors.

His first published work was a review of a stage performance, "Miss Maggie Mitchell in Fanchon the Cricket," published in 1863. About a year later, A Tragedy of Error, his first short story, was published anonymously. James's first payment was for an appreciation of Sir Walter Scott's novels, written for the North American Review. He wrote fiction and non-fiction pieces for The Nation and Atlantic Monthly, where Fields was editor. In 1871 he published his first novel, Watch and Ward, in serial form in the Atlantic Monthly. The novel was later published in book form in 1878.

During a 14-month trip through Europe in 1869–70 he met Ruskin, Dickens, Matthew Arnold, William Morris, and George Eliot. Rome impressed him profoundly. "Here I am then in the Eternal City," he wrote to his brother William. "At last—for the first time—I live!" He attempted to support himself as a freelance writer in Rome, then secured a position as Paris correspondent for the New York Tribune, through the influence of its editor John Hay. When these efforts failed he returned to New York City. During 1874 and 1875 he published Transatlantic Sketches, A Passionate Pilgrim, and Roderick Hudson. During this early period in his career he was influenced by Nathaniel Hawthorne.

In 1869 he settled in London. There he established relationships with Macmillan and other publishers, who paid for serial installments that they would later publish in book form. The audience for these serialized novels was largely made up of middle-class women, and James struggled to fashion serious literary work within the strictures imposed by editors' and publishers' notions of what was suitable for young women to read. He lived in rented rooms but was able to join gentlemen's clubs that had libraries and where he could entertain male friends. He was introduced to English society by Henry Adams and Charles Milnes Gaskell, the latter introducing him to the Travellers' and the Reform Clubs.

In the fall of 1875 he moved to the Latin Quarter of Paris. Aside from two trips to America, he spent the next three decades—the rest of his life—in Europe. In Paris he met Zola, Alphonse Daudet, Maupassant, Turgenev, and others. He stayed in Paris only a year before moving to London.

In England he met the leading figures of politics and culture. He continued to be a prolific writer, producing The American (1877), The Europeans (1878), a revision of Watch and Ward (1878), French Poets and Novelists (1878), Hawthorne (1879), and several shorter works of fiction. In 1878 Daisy Miller established his fame on both sides of the Atlantic. It drew notice perhaps mostly because it depicted a woman whose behavior is outside the social norms of Europe. He also began his first masterpiece, The Portrait of a Lady, which would appear in 1881.

In 1877 he first visited Wenlock Abbey in Shropshire, home of his friend Charles Milnes Gaskell whom he had met through Henry Adams. He was much inspired by the darkly romantic Abbey and the surrounding countryside, which features in his essay Abbeys and Castles. In particular the gloomy monastic fishponds behind the Abbey are said to have inspired the lake in The Turn of the Screw.

While living in London, James continued to follow the careers of the "French realists", Émile Zola in particular. Their stylistic methods influenced his own work in the years to come. Hawthorne's influence on him faded during this period, replaced by George Eliot and Ivan Turgenev. 1879–1882 saw the publication of The Europeans, Washington Square, Confidence, and The Portrait of a Lady. He visited America in 1882–1883, then returned to London.

The period from 1881 to 1883 was marked by several losses. His mother died in 1881, followed by his father a few months later, and then by his brother Wilkie. Emerson, an old family friend, died in 1882. His friend Turgenev died in 1883.

Middle years, 1884–1897

In 1884 James made another visit to Paris. There he met again with Zola, Daudet, and Goncourt. He had been following the careers of the French "realist" or "naturalist" writers, and was increasingly influenced by them. In 1886, he published The Bostonians and The Princess Casamassima, both influenced by the French writers he'd studied assiduously. Critical reaction and sales were poor. He wrote to Howells that the books had hurt his career rather than helped because they had "reduced the desire, and demand, for my productions to zero". During this time he became friends with Robert Louis Stevenson, John Singer Sargent, Edmund Gosse, George du Maurier, Paul Bourget, and Constance Fenimore Woolson. His third novel from the 1880s was The Tragic Muse. Although he was following the precepts of Zola in his novels of the '80s, their tone and attitude are closer to the fiction of Alphonse Daudet. The lack of critical and financial success for his novels during this period led him to try writing for the theatre. (His dramatic works and his experiences with theatre are discussed below.)

In the last quarter of 1889, he started translating "for pure and copious lucre" Port Tarascon, the third volume of Alphonse Daudet adventures of Tartarin de Tarascon. Serialized in Harper's Monthly Magazine from June 1890, this translation praised as "clever" by The Spectator was published in January 1891 by Sampson Low, Marston, Searle & Rivington.

After the stage failure of Guy Domville in 1895, James was near despair and thoughts of death plagued him. The years spent on dramatic works were not entirely a loss. As he moved into the last phase of his career he found ways to adapt dramatic techniques into the novel form.

In the late 1880s and throughout the 1890s James made several trips through Europe. He spent a long stay in Italy in 1887. In that year the short novel The Aspern Papers and The Reverberator were published.

Late years, 1898–1916

In 1897–1898 he moved to Rye, Sussex, and wrote The Turn of the Screw. 1899–1900 saw the publication of The Awkward Age and The Sacred

51

Fount. During 1902–1904 he wrote The Ambassadors, The Wings of the Dove, and The Golden Bowl.

In 1904 he revisited America and lectured on Balzac. In 1906–1910 he published The American Scene and edited the "New York Edition", a 24-volume collection of his works. In 1910 his brother William died; Henry had just joined William from an unsuccessful search for relief in Europe on what then turned out to be his (Henry's) last visit to the United States (from summer 1910 to July 1911), and was near him, according to a letter he wrote, when he died.

In 1913 he wrote his autobiographies, A Small Boy and Others, and Notes of a Son and Brother. After the outbreak of the First World War in 1914 he did war work. In 1915 he became a British subject and was awarded the Order of Merit the following year. He died on 28 February 1916, in Chelsea, London. As he requested, his ashes were buried in Cambridge Cemetery in Massachusetts.

Biographers

James regularly rejected suggestions that he should marry, and after settling in London proclaimed himself "a bachelor". F. W. Dupee, in several volumes on the James family, originated the theory that he had been in love with his cousin Mary ("Minnie") Temple, but that a neurotic fear of sex kept him from admitting such affections: "James's invalidism ... was itself the symptom of some fear of or scruple against sexual love on his part." Dupee used an episode from James's memoir A Small Boy and Others, recounting a dream of a Napoleonic image in the Louvre, to exemplify James's romanticism about Europe, a Napoleonic fantasy into which he fled.

Dupee had not had access to the James family papers and worked principally from James's published memoir of his older brother, William, and the limited collection of letters edited by Percy Lubbock, heavily weighted toward James's last years. His account therefore moved directly from James's childhood, when he trailed after his older brother, to elderly invalidism. As more material became available to scholars, including the diaries of contemporaries and hundreds of affectionate and sometimes erotic letters written by James to younger men, the picture of neurotic celibacy gave way to a portrait of a closeted homosexual.

Between 1953 and 1972, Leon Edel authored a major five-volume biography of James, which accessed unpublished letters and documents after Edel gained the permission of James's family. Edel's portrayal of James included the suggestion he was celibate. It was a view first propounded by critic Saul Rosenzweig in 1943. In 1996 Sheldon M. Novick published Henry James: The Young Master, followed by Henry James: The Mature Master (2007). The first book "caused something of an uproar in Jamesian circles" as it challenged the previous received notion of celibacy, a once-familiar paradigm in biographies of homosexuals when direct evidence was non-existent. Novick also criticised Edel for following the discounted Freudian interpretation of homosexuality "as a kind of failure." The difference of opinion erupted in a series of exchanges between Edel and Novick which were published by the online magazine Slate, with the latter arguing that even the suggestion of celibacy went against James's own injunction "live!"—not "fantasize!"

A letter James wrote in old age to Hugh Walpole has been cited as an explicit statement of this. Walpole confessed to him of indulging in "high jinks", and James wrote a reply endorsing it: "We must know, as much as possible, in our beautiful art, yours & mine, what we are talking about — & the only way to know it is to have lived & loved & cursed & floundered & enjoyed & suffered — I don't think I regret a single 'excess' of my responsive youth".

The interpretation of James as living a less austere emotional life has been subsequently explored by other scholars. The often intense politics of Jamesian scholarship has also been the subject of studies. Author Colm Tóibín has said that Eve Kosofsky Sedgwick's Epistemology of the Closet made a landmark difference to Jamesian scholarship by arguing that he be read as a homosexual writer whose desire to keep his sexuality a secret shaped his layered style and dramatic artistry. According to Tóibín such a reading "removed James from the realm of dead white males who wrote about posh people. He became our contemporary."

James's letters to expatriate American sculptor Hendrik Christian Andersen have attracted particular attention. James met the 27-year-old Andersen in Rome in 1899, when James was 56, and wrote letters to Andersen that are intensely emotional: "I hold you, dearest boy, in my innermost love, & count on your feeling me—in every throb of your soul". In a letter of 6 May 1904, to his brother William, James referred to himself as "always your hopelessly celibate even though sexagenarian Henry". How accurate that description might have been is the subject of contention among James's biographers,   but the letters to Andersen were occasionally quasi-erotic: "I put, my dear boy, my arm around you, & feel the pulsation, thereby, as it were, of our excellent future & your admirable endowment." To his homosexual friend Howard Sturgis, James could write: "I repeat, almost to indiscretion, that I could live with you. Meanwhile I can only try to live without you."

His numerous letters to the many young gay men among his close male friends are more forthcoming. In a letter to Howard Sturgis, following a long visit, James refers jocularly to their "happy little congress of two" and in letters to Hugh Walpole he pursues convoluted jokes and puns about their relationship, referring to himself as an elephant who "paws you oh so benevolently" and winds about Walpole his "well meaning old trunk". His letters to Walter Berry printed by the Black Sun Press have long been celebrated for their lightly veiled eroticism.

He corresponded in almost equally extravagant language with his many female friends, writing, for example, to fellow novelist Lucy Clifford: "Dearest Lucy! What shall I say? when I love you so very, very much, and see you nine times for once that I see Others! Therefore I think that—if you want it made clear to the meanest intelligence—I love you more than I love Others." To his New York friend Mary Cadwalader Jones: "Dearest Mary Cadwalader. I yearn over you, but I yearn in vain; & your long silence really breaks my heart, mystifies, depresses, almost alarms me, to the point even of making me wonder if poor unconscious & doting old Célimare [Jones's pet name for James] has 'done' anything, in some dark somnambulism of the spirit, which has ... given you a bad moment, or a wrong impression, or a 'colourable pretext' ... However these things may be, he loves you as tenderly as ever;

nothing, to the end of time, will ever detach him from you, & he remembers those Eleventh St. matutinal intimes hours, those telephonic matinées, as the most romantic of his life ..." His long friendship with American novelist Constance Fenimore Woolson, in whose house he lived for a number of weeks in Italy in 1887, and his shock and grief over her suicide in 1894, are discussed in detail in Edel's biography and play a central role in a study by Lyndall Gordon. (Edel conjectured that Woolson was in love with James and killed herself in part because of his coldness, but Woolson's biographers have objected to Edel's account.)

Works

Style and themes

James is one of the major figures of trans-Atlantic literature. His works frequently juxtapose characters from the Old World (Europe), embodying a feudal civilisation that is beautiful, often corrupt, and alluring, and from the New World (United States), where people are often brash, open, and assertive and embody the virtues—freedom and a more highly evolved moral character—of the new American society. James explores this clash of personalities and cultures, in stories of personal relationships in which power is exercised well or badly. His protagonists were often young American women facing oppression or abuse, and as his secretary Theodora Bosanquet remarked in her monograph Henry James at Work:

> When he walked out of the refuge of his study and into the world and looked around him, he saw a place of torment, where creatures of prey perpetually thrust their claws into the quivering flesh of doomed, defenseless children of light ... His novels are a repeated exposure of this wickedness, a reiterated and passionate plea for the fullest freedom of development, unimperiled by reckless and barbarous stupidity.

Critics have jokingly described three phases in the development of James's prose: "James I, James II, and The Old Pretender." He wrote short stories and plays. Finally, in his third and last period he returned to the long, serialised novel. Beginning in the second period, but most noticeably in the third, he increasingly abandoned direct statement in favour of frequent double negatives, and complex descriptive imagery. Single paragraphs began to run for page after page, in which an initial noun would be succeeded by pronouns surrounded by clouds of adjectives and prepositional clauses, far from their original referents, and verbs would be deferred and then preceded by a series of adverbs. The overall effect could be a vivid evocation of a scene as perceived by a sensitive observer. It has been debated whether this change of style was engendered by James's shifting from writing to dictating to a typist, a change made during the composition of What Maisie Knew.

In its intense focus on the consciousness of his major characters, James's later work foreshadows extensive developments in 20th century fiction. Indeed, he might have influenced stream-of-consciousness writers such as Virginia Woolf, who not only read some of his novels but also wrote essays about them. Both contemporary and modern readers have found the late style difficult and unnecessary; his friend Edith Wharton, who admired him greatly, said that there were passages in his work that were all but incomprehensible. James was harshly portrayed by H. G. Wells as a hippopotamus laboriously attempting to pick up a pea that had got into a corner of its cage. The "late James" style was ably parodied by Max Beerbohm in "The Mote in the Middle Distance".

More important for his work overall may have been his position as an expatriate, and in other ways an outsider, living in Europe. While he came from middle-class and provincial beginnings (seen from the perspective of European polite society) he worked very hard to gain access to all levels of society, and the settings of his fiction range from working class to aristocratic, and often describe the efforts of middle-class Americans to make their way in European capitals. He confessed he got some of his best story ideas from gossip at the dinner table or at country house weekends. He worked for a living, however, and lacked the experiences of select schools, university, and army service, the common bonds of masculine society. He was furthermore a man whose tastes and interests were, according to the prevailing standards of Victorian era Anglo-American culture, rather feminine, and who was shadowed by the cloud of prejudice that then and later accompanied suspicions of his homosexuality. Edmund Wilson famously compared James's objectivity to Shakespeare's:

One would be in a position to appreciate James better if one compared him with the dramatists of the seventeenth century—Racine and Molière, whom he resembles in form as well as in point of view, and even Shakespeare, when allowances are made for the most extreme differences in subject and form. These poets are not, like Dickens and Hardy, writers of melodrama—either humorous or pessimistic, nor secretaries of society like Balzac, nor prophets like Tolstoy: they are occupied simply with the presentation of conflicts of moral character, which they do not concern themselves about softening or averting. They do not indict society for these situations: they regard them as universal and inevitable. They do not even blame God for allowing them: they accept them as the conditions of life.

It is also possible to see many of James's stories as psychological thought-experiments. In his preface to the New York edition of The American he describes the development of the story in his mind as exactly such: the "situation" of an American, "some robust but insidiously beguiled and betrayed, some cruelly wronged, compatriot..." with the focus of the story being on the response of this wronged man. The Portrait of a Lady may be an experiment to see what happens when an idealistic young woman suddenly becomes very rich. In many of his tales, characters seem to exemplify alternative futures and possibilities, as most markedly in "The Jolly Corner", in which the protagonist and a ghost-doppelganger live alternative American and European lives; and in others, like The Ambassadors, an older James seems fondly to regard his own younger self facing a crucial moment.

Major novels

The first period of James's fiction, usually considered to have culminated in The Portrait of a Lady, concentrated on the contrast between Europe and America. The style of these novels is generally straightforward and, though personally characteristic, well within the norms of 19th-century fiction. Roderick Hudson (1875) is a Künstlerroman that traces the development of the title character, an extremely talented sculptor. Although the book shows some signs of immaturity—this was James's first serious attempt at a full-length novel—it has attracted favourable comment due to the vivid realisation of the three major characters: Roderick Hudson, superbly gifted but unstable and unreliable; Rowland Mallet, Roderick's limited but much more mature friend and patron; and Christina Light, one of James's most enchanting and maddening femmes fatales. The pair of Hudson and Mallet has been seen as representing the two sides of James's own nature: the wildly imaginative artist and the brooding conscientious mentor.

In The Portrait of a Lady (1881) James concluded the first phase of his career with a novel that remains his most popular piece of long fiction. The story is of a spirited young American woman, Isabel Archer, who "affronts her destiny" and finds it overwhelming. She inherits a large amount of money and subsequently becomes the victim of Machiavellian scheming by two American expatriates. The narrative is set mainly in Europe, especially in England and Italy. Generally regarded as the masterpiece of his early phase, The Portrait of a Lady is described as a psychological novel, exploring the minds of his characters, and almost a work of social science, exploring the differences between Europeans and Americans, the old and the new worlds.

The second period of James's career, which extends from the publication of The Portrait of a Lady through the end of the nineteenth century, features less popular novels including The Princess Casamassima, published serially in The Atlantic Monthly in 1885–1886, and The Bostonians, published serially in The Century Magazine during the same period. This period also featured James's celebrated Gothic novella, The Turn of the Screw.

The third period of James's career reached its most significant achievement in three novels published just around the start of the 20th century: The Wings of the Dove (1902), The Ambassadors (1903), and The Golden Bowl (1904). Critic F. O. Matthiessen called this "trilogy" James's major phase, and these novels have certainly received intense critical study. It was the second-written of the books, The Wings of the Dove (1902) that was the first published because it attracted no serialization. This novel tells the story of Milly Theale, an American heiress stricken with a serious disease, and her impact on the people around her. Some of these people befriend Milly with honourable motives, while others are more self-interested. James stated in his autobiographical books that Milly was based on Minny Temple, his beloved cousin who died at an early age of tuberculosis. He said that he attempted in the novel to wrap her memory in the "beauty and dignity of art".

Shorter narratives

James was particularly interested in what he called the "beautiful and blest nouvelle", or the longer form of short narrative. Still, he produced a number of very short stories in which he achieved notable compression of sometimes complex subjects. The following narratives are representative of James's achievement in the shorter forms of fiction.

- "A Tragedy of Error" (1864), short story
- "The Story of a Year" (1865), short story
- A Passionate Pilgrim (1871), novella
- Madame de Mauves (1874), novella
- Daisy Miller (1878), novella
- The Aspern Papers (1888), novella
- The Lesson of the Master (1888), novella
- The Pupil (1891), short story
- "The Figure in the Carpet" (1896), short story
- The Beast in the Jungle (1903), novella
- An International Episode (1878)
- Picture and Text
- Four Meetings (1885)
- A London Life, and Other Tales (1889)
- The Spoils of Poynton (1896)

- Embarrassments (1896)

- The Two Magics: The Turn of the Screw, Covering End (1898)

- A Little Tour of France (1900)

- The Sacred Fount (1901)

- Views and Reviews (1908)

- The Wings of the Dove, Volume I (1902)

- The Wings of the Dove, Volume II (1909)

- The Finer Grain (1910)

- The Outcry (1911)

- Lady Barbarina: The Siege of London, An International Episode and Other Tales (1922)

- The Birthplace (1922)

Plays

At several points in his career James wrote plays, beginning with one-act plays written for periodicals in 1869 and 1871 and a dramatisation of his popular novella Daisy Miller in 1882. From 1890 to 1892, having received a bequest that freed him from magazine publication, he made a strenuous effort to succeed on the London stage, writing a half-dozen plays of which only one, a dramatisation of his novel The American, was produced. This play was performed for several years by a touring repertory company and had a respectable run in London, but did not earn very much money for James. His other plays written at this time were not produced.

In 1893, however, he responded to a request from actor-manager George Alexander for a serious play for the opening of his renovated St. James's Theatre, and wrote a long drama, Guy Domville, which Alexander produced. There was a noisy uproar on the opening night, 5 January 1895, with hissing from the gallery when James took his bow after the final curtain, and the author was upset. The play received moderately good reviews and had a modest run of four weeks before being taken off to make way for Oscar Wilde's The Importance of Being Earnest, which Alexander thought would have better prospects for the coming season.

After the stresses and disappointment of these efforts James insisted that he would write no more for the theatre, but within weeks had agreed to write a curtain-raiser for Ellen Terry. This became the one-act "Summersoft", which he later rewrote into a short story, "Covering End", and then expanded into a full-length play, The High Bid, which had a brief run in London in 1907, when James made another concerted effort to write for the stage. He wrote three new plays, two of which were in production when the death of Edward VII on 6 May 1910 plunged London into mourning and theatres closed. Discouraged by failing health and the stresses of theatrical work, James did not renew his efforts in the theatre, but recycled his plays as successful novels. The Outcry was a best-seller in the United States when it was published in 1911. During the years 1890–1893 when he was most engaged with the theatre, James wrote a good deal of theatrical criticism and assisted Elizabeth Robins and others in translating and producing Henrik Ibsen for the first time in London.

Leon Edel argued in his psychoanalytic biography that James was traumatised by the opening night uproar that greeted Guy Domville, and that it plunged him into a prolonged depression. The successful later novels, in Edel's view, were the result of a kind of self-analysis, expressed in fiction, which partly freed him from his fears. Other biographers and scholars have not accepted this account, however; the more common view being that of F.O. Matthiessen, who wrote: "Instead of being crushed by the collapse of his hopes [for the theatre]... he felt a resurgence of new energy."

Non-fiction

Beyond his fiction, James was one of the more important literary critics in the history of the novel. In his classic essay The Art of Fiction (1884), he argued against rigid prescriptions on the novelist's choice of subject and method of treatment. He maintained that the widest possible freedom in content and approach would help ensure narrative fiction's continued vitality.

James wrote many valuable critical articles on other novelists; typical is his book-length study of Nathaniel Hawthorne, which has been the subject of critical debate. Richard Brodhead has suggested that the study was emblematic of James's struggle with Hawthorne's influence, and constituted an effort to place the elder writer "at a disadvantage." Gordon Fraser, meanwhile, has suggested that the study was part of a more commercial effort by James to introduce himself to British readers as Hawthorne's natural successor.

When James assembled the New York Edition of his fiction in his final years, he wrote a series of prefaces that subjected his own work to searching, occasionally harsh criticism.

At 22 James wrote The Noble School of Fiction for The Nation's first issue in 1865. He would write, in all, over 200 essays and book, art, and theatre reviews for the magazine.

For most of his life James harboured ambitions for success as a playwright. He converted his novel The American into a play that enjoyed modest returns in the early 1890s. In all he wrote about a dozen plays, most of which went unproduced. His costume drama Guy Domville failed disastrously on its opening night in 1895. James then largely abandoned his efforts to conquer the stage and returned to his fiction. In his Notebooks he maintained that his theatrical experiment benefited his novels and tales by helping him dramatise his characters' thoughts and emotions. James produced a small but valuable amount of theatrical criticism, including perceptive appreciations of Henrik Ibsen.

With his wide-ranging artistic interests, James occasionally wrote on the visual arts. Perhaps his most valuable contribution was his favourable assessment of fellow expatriate John Singer Sargent, a painter whose critical status has improved markedly in recent decades. James also wrote sometimes charming, sometimes brooding articles about various places he visited and lived in. His most famous books of travel writing include Italian Hours (an example of the charming approach) and The American Scene (most definitely on the brooding side).

James was one of the great letter-writers of any era. More than ten thousand of his personal letters are extant, and over three thousand have been published in a large number of collections. A complete edition of James's letters began publication in 2006, edited by Pierre Walker and Greg Zacharias. As of 2014, eight volumes have been published, covering the period from 1855 to 1880. James's correspondents included celebrated contemporaries like Robert Louis Stevenson, Edith Wharton and Joseph Conrad, along with many others in his wide circle of friends and acquaintances. The letters range from the "mere twaddle of graciousness" to serious discussions of artistic, social and personal issues.

Very late in life James began a series of autobiographical works: A Small Boy and Others, Notes of a Son and Brother, and the unfinished The Middle Years. These books portray the development of a classic observer who was passionately interested in artistic creation but was somewhat reticent about participating fully in the life around him.

Reception

Criticism, biographies and fictional treatments

James's work has remained steadily popular with the limited audience of educated readers to whom he spoke during his lifetime, and has remained firmly in the canon, but, after his death, some American critics, such as Van Wyck Brooks, expressed hostility towards James for his long expatriation and eventual naturalisation as a British subject. Other critics such as E. M. Forster complained about what they saw as James's squeamishness in the treatment of sex and other possibly controversial material, or dismissed his late style as difficult and obscure, relying heavily on extremely long sentences and excessively latinate language. Similarly Oscar Wilde criticised him for writing "fiction as if it were a painful duty". Vernon Parrington, composing a canon of American literature, condemned James for having cut himself off from America. Jorge Luis Borges wrote about him, "Despite the scruples and delicate complexities of James, his work suffers from a major defect: the absence of life." And Virginia Woolf, writing to Lytton Strachey, asked, "Please tell me what you find in Henry James. ... we have his works here, and

I read, and I can't find anything but faintly tinged rose water, urbane and sleek, but vulgar and pale as Walter Lamb. Is there really any sense in it?" The novelist W. Somerset Maugham wrote, "He did not know the English as an Englishman instinctively knows them and so his English characters never to my mind quite ring true," and argued "The great novelists, even in seclusion, have lived life passionately. Henry James was content to observe it from a window." Maugham nevertheless wrote, "The fact remains that those last novels of his, notwithstanding their unreality, make all other novels, except the very best, unreadable." Colm Tóibín observed that James "never really wrote about the English very well. His English characters don't work for me."

Despite these criticisms, James is now valued for his psychological and moral realism, his masterful creation of character, his low-key but playful humour, and his assured command of the language. In his 1983 book, The Novels of Henry James, Edward Wagenknecht offers an assessment that echoes Theodora Bosanquet's:

> "To be completely great," Henry James wrote in an early review, "a work of art must lift up the heart," and his own novels do this to an outstanding degree ... More than sixty years after his death, the great novelist who sometimes professed to have no opinions stands foursquare in the great Christian humanistic and democratic tradition. The men and women who, at the height of World War II, raided the secondhand shops for his out-of-print books knew what they were about. For no writer ever raised a braver banner to which all who love freedom might adhere.

William Dean Howells saw James as a representative of a new realist school of literary art which broke with the English romantic tradition epitomised by the works of Charles Dickens and William Makepeace Thackeray. Howells wrote that realism found "its chief exemplar in Mr. James... A novelist he is not, after the old fashion, or after any fashion but his own." F.R. Leavis championed Henry James as a novelist of "established pre-eminence" in The Great Tradition (1948), asserting that The Portrait of a Lady and The Bostonians were "the two most brilliant novels in the language." James is now prized as a master of point of view who moved literary fiction forward by insisting in showing, not telling, his stories to the reader. (Source: Wikipedia)

NOTABLE WORKS

NOVELS

Watch and Ward (1871)

Roderick Hudson (1875)

The American (1877)

The Europeans (1878)

Confidence (1879)

Washington Square (1880)

The Portrait of a Lady (1881)

The Bostonians (1886)

The Princess Casamassima (1886)

The Reverberator (1888)

The Tragic Muse (1890)

The Other House (1896)

The Spoils of Poynton (1897)

What Maisie Knew (1897)

The Awkward Age (1899)

The Sacred Fount (1901)

The Wings of the Dove (1902)

The Ambassadors (1903)

The Golden Bowl (1904)

The Whole Family (collaborative novel with eleven other authors, 1908)

The Outcry (1911)

The Ivory Tower (unfinished, published posthumously 1917)

The Sense of the Past (unfinished, published posthumously 1917)

SHORT STORIES AND NOVELLAS

A Tragedy of Error (1864)

The Story of a Year (1865)

A Landscape Painter (1866)

A Day of Days (1866)

My Friend Bingham (1867)

Poor Richard (1867)

The Story of a Masterpiece (1868)

A Most Extraordinary Case (1868)

A Problem (1868)

De Grey: A Romance (1868)

Osborne's Revenge (1868)

The Romance of Certain Old Clothes (1868)

A Light Man (1869)

Gabrielle de Bergerac (1869)

Travelling Companions (1870)

A Passionate Pilgrim (1871)

At Isella (1871)

Master Eustace (1871)

Guest's Confession (1872)

The Madonna of the Future (1873)

The Sweetheart of M. Briseux (1873)

The Last of the Valerii (1874)

Madame de Mauves (1874)

Adina (1874)

Professor Fargo (1874)

Eugene Pickering (1874)

Benvolio (1875)

Crawford's Consistency (1876)

The Ghostly Rental (1876)

Four Meetings (1877)

Rose-Agathe (1878, as Théodolinde)

Daisy Miller (1878)

Longstaff's Marriage (1878)

An International Episode (1878)

The Pension Beaurepas (1879)

A Diary of a Man of Fifty (1879)

A Bundle of Letters (1879)

The Point of View (1882)

The Siege of London (1883)

Impressions of a Cousin (1883)

Lady Barberina (1884)

Pandora (1884)

The Author of Beltraffio (1884)

Georgina's Reasons (1884)

A New England Winter (1884)

The Path of Duty (1884)

Mrs. Temperly (1887)

Louisa Pallant (1888)

The Aspern Papers (1888)

The Liar (1888)

The Modern Warning (1888, originally published as The Two Countries)

A London Life (1888)

The Patagonia (1888)

The Lesson of the Master (1888)

The Solution (1888)

The Pupil (1891)

Brooksmith (1891)

The Marriages (1891)

The Chaperon (1891)

Sir Edmund Orme (1891)

Nona Vincent (1892)

The Real Thing (1892)

The Private Life (1892)

Lord Beaupré (1892)

The Visits (1892)

Sir Dominick Ferrand (1892)

Greville Fane (1892)

Collaboration (1892)

Owen Wingrave (1892)

The Wheel of Time (1892)

The Middle Years (1893)

The Death of the Lion (1894)

The Coxon Fund (1894)

The Next Time (1895)

Glasses (1896)

The Altar of the Dead (1895)

The Figure in the Carpet (1896)

The Way It Came (1896, also published as The Friends of the Friends)

The Turn of the Screw (1898)

Covering End (1898)

In the Cage (1898)

John Delavoy (1898)

The Given Case (1898)

Europe (1899)

The Great Condition (1899)

The Real Right Thing (1899)

Paste (1899)

The Great Good Place (1900)

Maud-Evelyn (1900)

Miss Gunton of Poughkeepsie (1900)

The Tree of Knowledge (1900)

The Abasement of the Northmores (1900)

The Third Person (1900)

The Special Type (1900)

The Tone of Time (1900)

Broken Wings (1900)

The Two Faces (1900)

Mrs. Medwin (1901)

The Beldonald Holbein (1901)

The Story in It (1902)

Flickerbridge (1902)

The Birthplace (1903)

The Beast in the Jungle (1903)

The Papers (1903)

Fordham Castle (1904)

Julia Bride (1908)

The Jolly Corner (1908)

The Velvet Glove (1909)

Mora Montravers (1909)

Crapy Cornelia (1909)

The Bench of Desolation (1909)

A Round of Visits (1910)

OTHER

Transatlantic Sketches (1875)

French Poets and Novelists (1878)

Hawthorne (1879)

Portraits of Places (1883)

A Little Tour in France (1884)

Partial Portraits (1888)

Essays in London and Elsewhere (1893)

Picture and Text (1893)

Terminations (1893)

Theatricals (1894)

Theatricals: Second Series (1895)

Guy Domville (1895)

The Soft Side (1900)

William Wetmore Story and His Friends (1903)

The Better Sort (1903)

English Hours (1905)

The Question of our Speech; The Lesson of Balzac. Two Lectures (1905)

The American Scene (1907)

Views and Reviews (1908)

Italian Hours (1909)

A Small Boy and Others (1913)

Notes on Novelists (1914)

Notes of a Son and Brother (1914)

Within the Rim (1918)

Travelling Companions (1919)

Notebooks (various, published posthumously)

The Middle Years (unfinished, published posthumously 1917)

A Most Unholy Trade (1925, published posthumously)

The Art of the Novel : Critical Prefaces (1934)